The Other Side of the Looking Glass

L.E. Gibler

Published by BlytheLea Publishing

Tumwater, WA - USA

www.blytheleabooks.com

Library of Congress Control Number: 2021908342

ISBN: 1-7371281-0-6
ISBN-13: 978-1-7371281-0-6

DEDICATION

To my family and friends. For encouraging me, nagging me, and always believing.

ONE

When I was a child, my fondest memories were of World Walking with my grandmother. The ability to move between worlds through merely a Portal was a gift reserved for very few. I was one of the last of my family's line. In fact, as far as I knew, I was the very last of the Terres. This talent was passed intermittently from one generation to another. The problem was that we usually fell in love with regular humans. Their impure blood had weakened our line over generations. Once there were at least a thousand Walkers between worlds. Now, we were reduced to fewer than a hundred. In my world, there were three of us: me, my grandmother, and my father.

On my sixth birthday, my grandmother gave me a long, antique mirror that had passed for generations through our family. It was a Portal, a mirror with access to any number of worlds. One step through my Portal and we entered into a maze. Gilded mirrors lined a gravel path, trees arced around and the whole area spoke of a fairy tale shrouded in mist. There were lesser Portals in every one of the other Forty One Realms, but only a true Portal, in the hands of a Walker, opened into this sort of limbo. Every other opened merely into the realm for which it had been created. Some of theses worlds were like ours. Some were far different. In every one of them a single moment of time had altered the events to, in some cases, a point so drastically that dinosaurs existed. In another, the world was still in a perennial Dark Age. Each world was given a number by Walkers, and the number was engraved on the entrance Portal in a Walker's limbo. The realm we live as you know it is referred to as the Twelfth Realm. For years my very favorite was the Thirteenth Realm. It was nearly identical to ours, but everything in it was more beautiful. Each color was more pronounced, the skies were bluer, the trees greener, and to every last detail the world was more perfect. Even the people seemed to shimmer, flaws, if they did exist, seemed too right to be wrong. What was it, one might ask, about this world that held me so enthralled? Well, I think it all started on that fateful birthday.

The Thirteenth Realm was the easiest to get to. It was a turn away from my new Portal. There was something to be said for a first taste of the exotic. I had run ahead of my grandmother, too excited to be held back, and after slipping into this new world, I had come face to face with Ivan.

The difference between a Walker and the rest of humanity is that every human exists in every world, or at least the potential for them does. If a bystander follows us through, they might run into their alter ego. When a Walker enters a world, the world folds a space in it to adapt to us. It helped us survive. In my own world I had known Ivan Battuta; he lived down the street. We were the same age, but that was about all we had in common. His father had started a luxury cab service and made more money than he knew what to do with. My father, as a Walker, had a comfortable world ready for him without working, but we would never ascend the social stratosphere.

When I tumbled into this Thirteenth Realm, the Ivan I knew was hardly staring back at me. His hair was longer, his eyes a little sharper. Even as a child, I could tell the difference between the two.

"Who are you?" he asked.

I got to my feet, having tripped in my enthusiasm to cross thresholds. Looking around, I was startled to realize that the street I lived on here was literally polished. The boy in front of me was out of place. His clothes weren't perfect, his hair wasn't perfectly coifed. A true novice, I knew in an instant I was in a different world.

"I'm Nora," I said, extending my hand.

He watched me suspiciously a second later before taking my hand and shaking it. "I'm Ivan."

"I know."

"How?" he asked.

"You live down the street from me," I replied. "You and your parents and two brothers."

He frowned, eyes narrowing. "Huh. Never seen you before."

My grandmother came hurrying after me before I could say something more. "Nora, what are you doing, child?" She huffed to a halt beside me. "You need to take things slowly." She noticed Ivan and stopped short of her rather mild mannered lecture. Grandmère could lecture and make strong men cry, but she rarely raised her voice with me. "Hello."

He nodded to her, clearly wondering what was going on. "You new too?"

Grandmother's white eyebrows climbed steadily in her lightly wrinkled face. "You mean you don't know me?" she asked.

He shook his head. "Never seen either of you

"Well, then let me introduce myself. I am Alanna Terre. And you are?"

He seemed to be struggling with a desire to stick around or run, but he watched the two of us and decided we were alright. "Ivan." He threw out his chest and held out his hand.

"A pleasure, Ivan," said my grandmother smoothly. Her sharp gray eyes with just a hint of lavender, identical to mine, watched us both closely. "Why don't the two of you run up the next street to the park? I'll follow."

Ivan shrugged and turned to me. Holding out his hand, he waited patiently until I put mine in his before pulling me along after him. I had never had a friend like Ivan before that day. My father was a bit of a shut in. He and my mother loved each other at times to the exclusion of everything else, including me. I went to school, came home, and played with my toys. It was a lonely life, but now that I had my Portal and my grandmother from time to time, it was hardly boring. And now, to top everything else off, I had Ivan. We played until the sun went down that first day, and I went to visit him nearly every day after school for years to come. As I grew older, I could tell a few subtle differences. He never invited me to his home, only meeting me at the same street corner. He never introduced me to his friends or brothers. It was like I was another world to him, and he jealously kept me separate.

I summoned my courage to introduce myself to the Ivan of my world, and we were fast friends, too, but it was still different. As I grew older and a bit braver, Grandmère took me to more worlds. There were only a handful she let me in alone. Too many were too dangerous even for a Walker. Dinosaurs knew no difference between pterodactyl for dinner and a girl. The less advanced worlds tended to hunt down strangers and burn them, or worse, and two worlds had no humans at all. Another dozen were on the brink of war, some nuclear. In the end, there were seven worlds I comfortably walked between. Grandmère had warned me of getting lost and never finding a way home. I had been lost in the twenty-ninth world overnight before Father had found me. After that, I stuck to the Thirteenth and Eleventh, the two closest to mine. I had found four Ivans besides the two I was friends with. Every one of them knew me instantly to be different. I asked my grandmother about this, but she shook her head and just said some humans could tell we were slightly different. However, she never looked me in the eyes, and she avoided talk of our gift for hours after.

Life seemed all too wonderful for several years, but that all came crashing down two days before my twelfth birthday. The Ivan of my world and I were busy with our homework when my father came crashing into the house in a panic.

"Where is she?" he cried to me.

"Who?" I asked, getting to my feet and trying to come to him.

"Your mother? Where is Celeste?"

"It's only five, Dad, Mom shouldn't be home for another thirty minutes." But my words were in vain. He tore the house apart, only to be stopped by a phone call. I'll never forget the way the color drained straight out of his face. He dropped the receiver from his lifeless hands, and I had to pick it up and be told the horrible truth: Celeste Terre was dead.

There was no consoling my father after her death. He shut himself up for days without even eating. Luckily for me, Ivan of the Thirteenth Realm had taught me to pick locks. I managed to get him to eat dinner at least, but it was hard to carry on. Grandmère stayed with us for months, and Ivan of the Twelfth Realm tried to help, but it was hard to have anyone in the house with my father being the way he was. He was my secret, even from my world's Ivan. It would have been a relief to visit my other Ivan in that time, but I couldn't risk leaving my father. Nearly a month later, I finally braved the Portal, only to find Ivan was no longer waiting for me. I went back for a week straight, but he never showed. It hurt, but it had to be expected. When I was exiting the Portal at the end of a fruitless seven days searching, my father was waiting for me.

"What do you think you're doing, Alinora?" he asked sharply.

I jumped to see him. It was rare enough that he left his room, but his appearance was truly frightening. His hair had grown longer, past his jaw bone and fast approaching his shoulders, and it was only lightly groomed, falling in shaggy dark snarls around an equally unkempt beard.

"World Walking," I replied. "How are you feeling today, Daddy?"

He ignored me and went to stand in front of the mirror. "All this world ever brought me was despair. It won't bring her back, it won't bring anyone back."

I reached out to touch him, but he shook me off.

"I never should have let Mother give this to you. You cannot understand. We are abominations, and we should be stopped!" I watched in horror as he brought his fist crashing through my mirror.

"Daddy!" I leaped to him, but the mirror was in pieces. I took his hand in mine, noticing the cuts. "We should go to the hospital," I said. "Come on." He seemed lost then. All his anger had been directed at the mirror and was now spent. I tried hard not to dwell on what he had done, focusing all my thought on managing to get him to the hospital on my own. He needed six stitches in his hand. When we finally came home, I took the mirror and pushed it under my bed, hoping that if it were out of sight, maybe my father might get it out of his mind.

Though my grandmother had helped to take care of my father in the months directly following my mother's death, she had wandered off after. She and my father never spoke when they were in the house together, and she seemed constrained as to what to say to me. The only day a year I was guaranteed to see her was my birthday.

The ache of that year slowly eased in the time that followed. By the time I was fifteen, my father and I could get through a day without any problems. He even started to care about his appearance and went out to work at a job he never explained to me. It didn't bother me, I was only too happy to have him back. Ivan of my world was allowed to visit on school nights for homework, and it was enough.

The one small problem with my father's job was that he would be gone for days without any word to me other than a note on the fridge about what credit card to use to order food. On those days, I longed for my grandmother. She, at least, could have offered some reasonable steadiness. When it became more widely known that I lived alone for frequent stints, it made me quite popular at school. The most popular girls, led by Jacqueline Sullen, quickly attached themselves to me. However, when it became equally apparent that I wasn't going to give in and have a party, my popularity waned again. Ivan, as always, was there to comfort me.

The length of my father's absences stretched from days to weeks as my junior year in high school progressed. I had once tried private schooling, but life was just as awkward at a private school as at public, and when Ivan enrolled at Columbia High, so did I. It was just like any other school, slightly run down halls and lockers that had seen fresh paint to cover all the graffiti. At least by my junior year I could drive myself, and I had my own bank account that was always full despite my not having a job. However, my father's absence did not go unnoticed by just my classmates. Teachers asked for an interview, classmates continued to ask for sleepovers. I didn't know what to tell them. I became famous for "I'll let you know". Anyone coming to ask me a question would walk away answering for themselves with those exact words. It was hard for a sixteen year old to get through high school on a good day. It was harder now with the continued pressure. I wanted so badly to escape into another world, but that option had been destroyed five years ago. I was stuck here, and I had to make the best of it.

The warm California weather was changing to brisker winds and cooler nights as October neared. It had been two weeks since I last saw my father, and even I was beginning to wonder. My birthday was only a few days away, and I had to hope he wouldn't forget. I couldn't be certain, and that hurt most of all. Ivan noticed my melancholy that day at school, and he followed me closely.

"Still home alone?" he asked gently, helping me get books from my locker.

I nodded, squinting at the four he held before putting two back. I was not an organized creature. My locker was filled to the brim with books and binders. It was something of a challenge to open the door without everything coming out at me. Ivan always stood to one side. He knew what might be coming.

"How long has it been?" he asked as I pried a binder out of the mess.

"Over two weeks."

"Do you think he'll be home by Friday?"

I smiled at him, my heart in my eyes. Trust Ivan to remember my birthday even if everyone else forgot. "I hope."

"Well, my mom has already made plans for us. She's got a caterer and everything." He took another step back as I readied to shut my locker.

"You shouldn't have," I said, throwing my

entire body weight into the door. It took two tries before I heard a satisfying click.

He shrugged and handed my books back over. "She worries about you. And with the move coming, she doesn't know what's going to happen when we leave."

I stopped mid stride and two students behind me bounced off my back. "What?"

His olive face flushed. "I told you last week, Nora. Dad got a promotion for L.A. We'll be leaving after quarter finals."

Everything seemed to come to a halt. The world was moving around me, but I wasn't. In fact, my brain wasn't working at all. I had stopped breathing, my heart had stopped beating. My world was crashing down and I couldn't get a grasp as to how to get it going again. Ivan watched me, clearly uncomfortable, but he didn't seem to know any better than me what to say.

"I thought you meant you were going on a business trip," I said, still not quite able to muster any depth to my words. They came out as an echo.

"No," he replied, becoming obviously panicked. "I'm sorry, I thought you took it really well at the time. I should have said something."

Nodding absently, I adjusted my bag across my shoulder and turned to our next class. "Well, it is what it is." However, someone was standing in front of us. I was forced to stop again as Jackie, the queen bee, waited for me to acknowledge her. She was flanked by her posse of Amber, Lara, and Krystal.

"Hey Nora."

I was too rattled to manage anything reasonable. "What do you want?"

She started slightly at my bluntness. "Well, a couple of friends and I were looking to have a party at Mimi's, but your place is so much bigger."

"Sorry---"

"But we would make sure to bring the best food. After all, it is your birthday this weekend."

"You know," said Ivan, "my mom would appreciate it. With all the movers, we're having to work around them to have the party."

I glared at my best friend. Sometimes I missed my other Ivan. This Ivan was a little more driven to be popular. "Is your mom going to come?"

He shrugged. "Sure. It could work."

Jackie smiled broadly and came over to run her arm through Ivan's. "It will work. It'll be perfect. So, what does your mom have planned?"

I felt a double sense of betrayal as I watched them walk off to class. Not only had I just been reminded of something I had intentionally forgotten because it was too painful, but now my party would go from being a comfortable experience to being something taken over by the in-crowd. My mind jumped to all of the movies made about parties gone wrong, and I had the sinking suspicion that was going to happen to me.

TWO

School could not be over soon enough. I bolted
from Chemistry to my car and left before half of the
school had even exited. Hoping against all hope, I
let myself in the house and searched from top to
bottom for my father. No one was there.
Depressed beyond thought, I decided to forgo my
homework in lieu of chocolate cake and a movie.
By four o'clock, I was comfortably ensconced in my
favorite flannel pjs, milk and cake to one side, and
my ultimate self pity movie, *Beauty and the Beast*,
playing on the old television set. I was barely to
the second musical number when the door bell
rang. Annoyed, I wanted to ignore the intrusion,
but it was obvious I was home. Unfolding myself
from my cocoon, I went to the door and opened it a
crack.

"Can I help you?" I asked, slightly surprised to
see someone who I didn't know. I had expected
Ivan or, worse case scenario, Jackie. Instead, I was
staring at a stranger. He was at least six feet, with
deep russet hair and hazel eyes. I stared into those
eyes, vaguely uneasy by their familiarity.

"Nora Terre?" he asked.

"Yes."

"I'm looking for your father. Is he home?"

"No, he won't be home until after work," I replied, knowing it wasn't a complete lie.

"And when would that be?"

I frowned uneasily. "Beats me. He gets here when he gets here. Could be twenty minutes, could be two hours." Or two weeks, but I refused to add that.

"Well, when he gets home, please let him know I stopped by." He smoothly handed a business card through the crack in the door. I watched him leave before throwing all three dead bolts. I edgily went about the house locking windows and doors. I didn't have an alarm system, and it seemed like a horrible shortcoming at that moment. My movie was ruined for me, as was my cake. I had lost all appetite. Cautiously, I crept up to my bedroom which had a view of the street. Peeking out, I saw the man sitting two houses down. Terror does funny things to a person. I couldn't think straight for a good two minutes. Finally, I managed to free some amount of common sense. I had to think of something. I went back downstairs for my cell phone. Of all things, it still worked. I would have thought that even a Walker would have a problem with cell phone plans, but apparently not. I called my grandmother first, but I was hardly surprised when she didn't answer. It was perfectly plausible that she was in another world. I left a message and then promptly chewed off the nail on my thumb. When it was bleeding at the quick, I called the only other person I could trust enough to help.

"Nora?"

"Ivan, I need your help."

"What is it? What's wrong?" His voice grew slightly panicked at the change of mine.

"There's this man who is waiting for my father. He's staking out the house. He's been here for the last two hours, I think. What time is it?"

"Five thirty."

"Okay, less than two hours, but I don't think he's going to leave until my father shows up."

"But you don't know when that will be."

I sighed in frustration, barely restraining a growl. "I know that. That's why I need your help. You have a car, right?"

"Yes," he hedged.

"You're a guy."

"What does that have to…" he trailed off.

"Chances are this guy doesn't really know my dad that well or he wouldn't be waiting two blocks down for him," I said, my voice growing more and more strained. "All I need is a male presence to arrive." That sounded so sexist, and it should have insulted my own sense of worth, but it was the truth. If I had lived alone with a rather absent mother, I would have probably begged Ivan's mom to come by for the same reason.

"Nora, your father is nearly twice my size."

"So improvise!"

"Alright, alright. I'll be over in about half an hour. Call me if he comes back before then."

"Thanks, Ivan."

"Sure thing."

I found a baseball bat in the basement, and was armed when the door bell rang again. I left the chain on when I opened the door a crack.

"Jeez, Nora, let me in before something falls off

of me."

I hurried to do just that. When he was safely in the entry hall, I threw the bolts again and turned to take in his appearance. He had collapsed on the stairwell and was painfully removing his boots. I hurried to help.

"Who knew my mother's feet were so big," he muttered. It took some work to wiggle his feet free, and he moaned when they were free. I held one boot up, realizing they were platforms.

"What are these, left over from the eighties?"

"Probably. My mom doesn't throw much out. And they worked." He was still grumbling as he pulled the jacket off. I was amazed at just how ingenious he had been. He had been right. Compared to my father, Ivan was half his size. A good two inches short of six feet with a slender form, he was almost feminine in his build. My father, on the other hand, was easily six feet with shoulders that were broad enough to hold the weight of the world. Their hair was their only similarity. The long dark locks that Ivan groomed so meticulously were shinier and better kept, but my father had never gotten back into the habit of regular hair cuts after my mother's death.

When Ivan handed me the jacket, I nearly fell over from the weight. He had stuffed the shoulders with socks, the middle had been stuffed with cardboard and tissue. The bottom had been weighted. Noticing the fishing weights, I peered curiously at it.

"To keep the coat from flying up in the wind," he replied with a sigh. "It was the only coat I had that would cover the changes. Technically it's my father's. I don't think he'll notice. It might be from the eighties too. No offense, but your father never seemed to care that much about his appearance."

I shrugged and put the coat away. "He doesn't." I turned back to see him trying to smooth his hair and had to hide an ill timed chuckle. Ivan would always care about his appearance. "Thanks, Ivan. This means the world to me."

He smiled a little lopsidedly. "Hey, I owe you. I'm sorry I didn't tell you sooner about the move."

"You did," I replied. "I just didn't want to listen."

His smile faded in a second. "Are you going to be okay?"

"I'll be fine."

"Honestly, Nora. What happens when I leave? What if your father doesn't come back?"

No matter what world I was in, Ivan had always known me better than sometimes I knew myself. I collapsed onto the stair next to him. He put his arms around me, and I let myself cry. "I don't know," I said around hiccups. My crying was abnormal. It came in one giant wave and then left, leaving hiccups in its wake. "I just don't know."

He squeezed my shoulder. "Come with us. Mom wouldn't have a problem with it. Neither would Dad. They're both worried about you."

I shook my head, warmed by the concern in his dark eyes. "I can't leave. If my father comes home, he'll never find me."

"You could leave a note."

"He wouldn't get it. Or if he did, what's to say he would even know where Los Angeles is? Most days he doesn't even know how to tie his own tie."

"Just think about it."

I let the conversation end there. I could never

leave my father, even if he wasn't home. Ivan knew it, too, but it meant so much to hear the offer. Sometimes I felt like everyone forgot that I even existed. It felt divine to be proven wrong. I ordered pizza for dinner, but we kept away from the windows. However, the man in the car didn't come back.

"So, who is he?" asked Ivan after a routine glance out the nearest window. "The guy in the black sedan, right?"

"Yeah, that's him, and I don't know. He left a card, but I was too rattled to care. I'll go get it."

Honestly, I didn't remember what I had done with the card. Back tracking through the house, I finally found it on the floor of the entry hall. As I bent to retrieve it, I felt like I was being watched. My hand stretched out for the baseball bat I had left in the entry hall. A shadow moved at the front door, visible through the frosted glass of the slit window. I nearly screamed, but something held me back. Clutching the bat with a death like grip, I slunk around into the living room where the largest window was. I dropped down behind the sofa that sat in front of the big bay window, edging up inch by inch to peer outside. Sure enough, there was a shadow of a man standing at the street corner. My house was one from the end of the block, and while there were a million reasons for that person to be standing there, I just knew, possibly fueled by paranoia, that it was someone watching me. Shaking from head to toe, I slunk back upstairs where Ivan was still in the entertainment room watching reruns on Comedy Network. He looked up and at the sight of me he leaped up with a grace that was natural to him and ran to my side.

"Are you okay, Nora? You look like you've seen a ghost."

I numbly handed over the business card and let him lead me to the couch. "There's someone out front," I managed past tingling lips.

Ivan held onto me as I collapsed into the plush comfort. "That makes sense. Look, I called home, they know I'm staying the night. My mom says to call if we want her here too."

I felt an absurd laugh bubbling in my throat, and unable to contain the near hysteria, it escaped. He had released me and was in the process of tucking me in like a baby, but he stopped at my odd outburst.

"What's so funny?"

"How many people do you know that would think it a good thing that you are staying over? I mean, really, what would anyone else think?"

He frowned, oddly offended, and went to sit away from me as a result. "My mother knows we're not friends like that," he replied tersely.

His words cut through me, through the ill timed humor to the still present fear. I knew I wasn't perfect, I had a slight gap between my front teeth, when I was really nervous I had a tendency to stutter, and I was a few pounds over the ideal weight, but that didn't mean it didn't hurt to be told by your best friend that you weren't attractive. It hurt even more when he noticed my changed expression and flushed.

"I didn't mean it like that, Nora. You know that."

"Do I?" I replied miserably. "No doubt if anyone at school heard, they'd think the same thing your mother does."

"You won't say anything, will you?"

That hurt more than anything else. Tears were welling in my eyes, and I wanted to lock myself in my bedroom and feel sorry for myself in reminiscence of my father. Years changed people, but the ridiculous thought entered my mind that my other Ivan, the one of the Thirteenth Realm, he wouldn't be so concerned about popularity that he would be afraid of spending the night.

"I won't tell anyone," I said quietly, having to force every syllable past my lips. "Thanks for staying despite the possible consequences." I got to my feet and padded off to my room. I wanted him to follow, oh how desperately did I want him to, but he didn't come. I curled up on my bed even though it wasn't even nine and cried myself to sleep.

I was up early. The sun was just beginning to break the horizon. In a sudden flash of terror, I realized I hadn't done an ounce of homework the night before. Forgetting everything else that had gone wrong, I bolted down the stairs in a mad rush only to find that Ivan was up as well. He smiled somewhat sheepishly when he saw me and went back to flipping pancakes.

"I figured your dad would be up early," he said by way of explanation. "Does he ever take you to school?"

Slightly stunned, I sat down at the kitchen bar. "Not since before my mother died," I said. "Usually I took the bus until I was able to drive."

He nodded, he had known most of this, but I guess he hadn't paid as much attention as his mother had. She had volunteered to drive me when something came up. Before this latest barb could pierce my fragile, self pitying heart, he put a plate of pancakes in front of me with powdered sugar. A small smile flickered on his face.

"Just the way you like them," he said with an apologizing smile and my heart melted. He was my best friend for a reason. In that second the previous night's emotional roller coaster was forgotten, and I managed not to start one too early in the morning either.

"Thanks, Ivan. You really didn't have to."

He shrugged and served up his plate. "What do you usually do for breakfast?"

"Cereal or Pop Tarts."

"And lunch?" he asked.

"I eat at the school. Dinner is usually TV dinners or take out. I've told myself I should learn to cook, but I've never managed to convince myself."

He smiled a little lopsidedly as he doused his pancakes in syrup. "You really should have taken Food and Nutrition with me last year. Everything I learned I learned in that class."

I laughed, knowing it for fact. His mother was a wonderful person, but she was not a cook. She had once told me that working as a cook/waitress for ten years from the time she was sixteen had taken away any interest in cooking she could have had after her husband made his money.

"Hindsight is 20/20, right?" I asked before taking my first bite.

"Right."

I pulled out my Calculus as we ate. He noticed, but other than raising his eyebrows, he didn't stop to talk. Writing with my left hand and eating with my right, I managed to finish up the ten problems that had been assigned. He thoughtfully cleared our plates as I delved into my History. He wandered off, and I hurried through the three essay questions before pulling out my Chemistry. I knew I was looking at vanishing time to finish, but somehow I managed. He came back, fully dressed in his usual apparel, designer jeans and a button down. When he was really wanting to make a statement he added a jacket and a scarf. He had gone to Europe the summer before and liked to model himself off of the Europe Chic. He looked good in it, but then I think he would look good in a paper bag. I, on the other hand, would look like a nightmare.

"We've got fifteen minutes to go. Do you want me to leave before you?"

I thought about this, but shook my head. "No, I think it would be best if we left together. I can even get a slight head start. Have you checked?"

He knew what I meant and nodded. "Car's still there. Where does your dad work?"

I shrugged. "Beats me. He never said anything about it. I just know he travels a lot. Obviously."

"Obviously," he agreed. "Well, I'll drive to the Park and Ride and see about catching a bus to school."

"I can follow, park a few blocks up and wait. I really don't like the idea of leaving you alone. I don't know who these people are or what they want."

He smiled, coming to stand beside me. "I appreciate the concern, but I think I can manage. The Park and Ride on Seventh is packed this time of day. They won't be able to tell me from the pack.

Though, I'll be forgoing the boots. Hopefully they don't notice my height difference."

Impulsively, I leaned over and kissed his cheek. "You're too good to me."

Surprisingly, he reached out and touched my cheek. "You deserve more than you have, including more from me. I know I haven't been the best of friends this year. And I'm leaving, so that makes me a total cad, but I promise, I'll do whatever I can to help." His thumb reached up to brush away a tear. "Go on, we're going to be late."

"Right." I bolted upstairs and was dressed in record time. He had thoughtfully packed my bags, and stood waiting for me at the entry. "You don't have a security system, do you?"

I shook my head. "I've got locks."

"Well, come on, no sense being upset about it. Are you going first?"

"I think that would be best. Here," I handed him a key. "Lock the first two. I lost the key for the bottom one." I hesitated a second as his hand met mine. I felt true fear and love in the same breath. "Take care, Ivan. Call me if anything happens. I won't leave the car until you get to school."

He smiled that endearingly crooked grin. "You worry too much, Nora."

I bit my lip, but kept anything more to myself. The next half hour was one of the tensest of my life. I could feel the pancakes begging to be let out of my stomach as the acid level rose to a near unbearable level, but before I could ruin my breakfast, Ivan knocked on my car window.

"Come on, we're going to be late."

School was more nerve racking than usual. I could barely focus, and it wasn't as if I was in any easy classes. However, as most of my teachers knew by now my family state, I was pretty sure they would think anything that was off was off because of my father's continued absence. Jackie approached me again about the party, but I managed to avoid any actual answers. Answers Ivan seemed only too willing to provide. By the end of the day, it seemed my party was a set thing, and by the talk, it was going to be bigger than my worst nightmare.

At lunch I tried to convince Ivan that it would be more odd than normal if he played my father being home two nights in a row, but he wouldn't listen to my arguments. Sometimes he had the stubbornness of a mule. Unlike me, Ivan was, if not popular, at least socially acceptable on a daily basis, and his afternoon had been planned in advance, so I made the trek alone with no immediate back up. There was no car waiting at the corner, and I felt a moment's relief until I made it up to the top step to see another business card sticking out. Hurrying inside, I dropped my bag and nearly felt my heart explode. Someone was in the kitchen. Taking my baseball bat, I tiptoed towards the noise. I have no idea how I managed, but as I rounded the corner, the bat dropped out of my lifeless fingers.

"Dad?"

He had turned at the clatter from the bat. His hair was neatly groomed, there was no beard, and he looked happy. I scarcely recognized him.

"Why hello, Nora, darling, how have you been?"

Reasoning was not the strongest of my virtues, sadly. "I have to make a call," I said a bit shortly, my voice a good octave higher than usual.

"What's wrong, Nora?" he asked, coming around to grab a hold of me before I could bolt.

"What's wrong? Th-that's wh-what you ask wh-when you've been gone for nearly three weeks?" I nearly screamed, my emotions starting to overpower long ago learned speech patterns to combat a mild stammer. I forced a deep breath, and then another before I thought it safe to continue. "Look, I need to call Ivan, tell him he doesn't need to come over."

My father's cheerfulness vanished in an instant, and the veiled darkness reminded me of the night he had broken my Portal. "Why is Ivan coming over?"

"Are you kidding?" I cried, backing away even as he held on. "I've been living here alone, I needed some back up, especially when someone sh-showed up to t-t-talk to you."

His expression turned even darker. "Who was it?"

I looked down at his hand on my arm. He was squeezing so tight I was positive I would have a bruise. "I don't know. He left a card." I held out the card that had been in the door. My father finally let go of me to look at it, letting out a blue streak a mile wide that would have amazed the saltiest of sailors.

"When did he come?"

"Last night. Ivan came by to make it look like you were home."

He nodded. "Bring him over again, I have to take care of something."

I was astounded as he headed for the back door. "You're leaving already?"

"I have to take care of this."

"B-but you just got back!"

"This is important, Nora."

He was out the door before I could say another word. I leaned against the arch way. "'I'm important,' I whispered to myself. Absently, I locked the doors of the house and checked the windows. Despite my discomfort, I managed to finish my homework before the sound of the front door opening startled me.

"Nora, I'm here," called out Ivan.

I peered around the corner to the landing. "Hey, you'll never guess who was here when I got home."

"The man currently parked across the street?" he asked, dropping his rigged trench coat. I had to admire Ivan. He had picked up a lot from Foods and from the Theater Class he was in now. He might not take the harder classes, but he was easily as smart as I was.

"No, my father."

He had started to hang up the coat, but he dropped it with a cacophony of odd noises and turned back to me. "Really?"

"Really. He ran out, though, as soon as I told him about our stalker."

"God, I'm so sorry, Nora."

It wasn't until he said something about it that I realized how hurt I should have felt about everything going on. A moment of self pity surfaced before I shook it away. "It's nothing he hasn't done before," I said with forced lightness. "Come on, I heated up some taquitos."

He visibly shuddered, but didn't fight the food I put before him. "You really need to eat some decent food," he said between mouthfuls. "Maybe you really should come with us to L.A. Sofia, our cook, would feed you like a queen. But you'd be getting some valuable things like vegetables in the process."

"You sound like a mother," I replied tartly.

"Someone should," he replied.

"Well, if my dad comes back, and stays for more than fifteen seconds, I'll talk to him about hiring a cook."

"Talk to him about coming with us," he pressed. "Really, Nora, you're like family anyway."

"Maybe. I'll let you know."

Oh no you don't," he said, shaking a taquito at me. "You don't get to put me off like you do everyone else. I won't give up on asking."

I shrugged, not knowing what to say. "I'm not trying to put you off, but I can't just vanish. I would need to talk to someone in my family. My grandmother should be here on Friday. Maybe she knows where my dad goes."

He wanted to argue, I could see it on his face, but he let it slide. "Well, what's the movie selection for tonight?"

"Whatever you want. Did you finish your homework?"

"Now who's sounding like a mother?"

I went to my room first, looking for another sweater. I got cold easily, my mother had once said I had at least inherited that from her. My hair and eyes were my grandmother's, blond hair and purple-gray eyes. My nose was anyone's guess, but it was pretty all the same. My mouth was also a mystery. Though my chin was definitely my father's and my heart shaped face was also his. It was a horrible thought, but I had often wondered if I had resembled my mother more if my father would have noticed me more after her death. As I came around my bed, I noticed an envelope just peeking out from the dust ruffle. Even though my locker was a mess, the lack of organization in my room was predominantly limited to my closet. Leaning down, I reached under my bed to pull out the envelope, but jerked back in pain and surprise. A tiny cry escaped me as I looked at the blood falling from my finger. It was then that I remembered the Portal I had hidden all those years ago. Reaching down again, to find the edges, I was startled back at the sudden bright lights coming from under my bed. It was like a sunrise under the mattress. I must have made some noise, for I could hear Ivan coming down the hall.

"Nora, are you okay?" he asked. Before I could answer, he was in the doorway, and his surprise mirrored my own. "What is under there?"

"My Portal," I replied, a little shocked. Getting to my feet, I tried to lift my mattress. Without a word between us, he came over to lift the other side. Under the box springs the most amazing thing was taking place. The pieces of my Portal were melding back together in a brilliant light show. We stood in mute amazement watching until the lights faded, leaving a complete mirror in their place.

"What is that?" Ivan asked in shock.

"It's a Portal," I said, carefully pushing the mirror out from under the bed. It was smaller than I remembered. He helped me prop the mirror against the dresser.

"But what's a Portal?"

"I'll show you." Grabbing his hand, I pulled him through. However, the breaking of the glass hadn't been kind to my Portal. Rather than the maze I had once entered, we walked right into another world. Technically speaking, we walked right into a closet. Opening the door, I was floored to find myself in my bedroom. Stepping out, I held out my hand to help Ivan. He was looking around in amazement.

"What is this place?"

"It's another world," I replied. "There are forty two Realms in total. We live in the Twelfth Realm."

He opened his mouth several times, but no further questions came out for several seconds. "Then what realm is this?"

"I don't know." I led him down the stairs. No one was home here, either, but there were signs of life. Letting us out, I looked up at the sky and the brilliant blue answered his question. "We're in the Thirteenth Realm," I said.

"Oh." He followed more for lack of something better to do than anything else. "Is this normal?"

"No," I said with a smile, pulling him along. "My father, my grandmother, and I are called Walkers. We can move between the Realms without detection."

"Do I exist here?" he asked, his head swiveling and taking in everything from the sidewalk to the clouds in the sky.

No one had ever covered taking a normal human along with me. I had to wonder about life altering paradoxes, but I couldn't bring myself to lie.

"You did."

He frowned at me, letting me lead him around

a lamp post. "Did? Am I dead here?"

"No, at least not that I know of. It's just I haven't been back since just after my mother died." I shuddered. "My father broke my Portal just afterwards. I guess what we saw was the Portal fixing itself. But it didn't finish, I used to be able to go to any number of places. All of the worlds were open to visit, but it seems I'm limited now."

"Nora," he said with heart stopping seriousness, "you are telling me the truth, aren't you? This isn't some sort of illusion? I'm not hallucinating, am I?"

"No. It's all real."

"Well, that's comforting, I guess. How do we get back?"

"The same way we came."

"Oh, good. Let's go then."

I was slightly disappointed as he turned and headed back without me. However, I knew I had to follow. And it was a lot to ask of him to take this all in so quickly. I should have told him, but when I was young, it had been my secret, and he hadn't been the friend he was now. Then, when he was my friend, there had been my mother's death. After that, with no Portal, it had seemed pointless. This secret had become lost and buried. Now it was overwhelming Ivan. I felt for him, truly I did. We didn't speak as I let us back in the house and we made our way up to my room that wasn't really my room. He walked through the Portal without me, but when I came through, he was waiting.

"You'll explain this all, right?" he asked, his voice strained.

"Ask me anything."

"Not right now. Later."

I was left alone. I knew he needed the space, and I respected that. We stayed apart all night. I kept waiting, but he never said a word. Even over breakfast, he said little more than a handful of words. As we prepared to leave, though, he took my hand in his.

"After school, could you take me again?"

I nodded. "I would love to."

"And then maybe you'll tell me what is going on?"

I smiled. "As much as I know."

He nodded, content. "Well, see you at school, then."

"See you."

I eagerly anticipated the end of my day all through classes. Ivan didn't avoid me, instead he seemed intent on staying near me. I was positive this was going to be perfect. I had never shared a secret of this magnitude before. It was all a bit heady to take in. After school, he went to his car and I headed home, still too giddy to worry about the rest of my problems. I went to stare at my Portal first thing, but I wanted to wait and share it with Ivan. As I stood there, I could see the envelope in my reflection. Reaching back down, I picked it up, recognizing my grandmother's handwriting. Curious, I began to open it when a loud crashing sound rang out below. Bolting to the top of the stairs, I saw Ivan on the floor.

"Ivan!" I ran down the stairs, skipping them in threes. "Are you alright?"

He jumped up before I could get to him and threw himself against the door, throwing the bolts as a solid form hit it from the other side. "Go upstairs, Nora!" I could hear the angry pounding and I felt a deeper fear than anything I had felt in the last seventy two hours, and that was saying something.

"Aren't you coming?" I asked in a shaky voice.

Instead of answering, he grabbed my hand and pulled me along. "Come on."

When we were in my room, He slammed it shut, dragging my bed across to sit in front of it. "Look, Nora, I am so sorry. I didn't realize what was happening until it was too late."

"What's going on?" I asked, feeling panic induced bile rise in my throat as I could hear a window breaking down stairs.

"I told Jackie about the mirror. I'm so sorry, Nora."

"But, I don't understand."

He grasped me on either side of my shoulders, shaking me slightly. "Her father is the one who has been hanging around. He knows something, and he followed me here. They nearly caught me at the bus station, but I managed to get away."

They were now coming up the stairs. I thought my heart would fail. "But what do they want?"

"To find your father. I don't understand it all, but they know about World Walkers, and they want to get you too. Now, go, Nora. You can make it to that other world. I'll break the mirror after you go."

"What? No, Ivan, you'll be hurt. Come with me."

He shook his head vehemently. "No, if I do that, they'll follow there as well. I called everyone in my family on the way over. All I have to do is hold them off a few minutes and I'll be okay. It's you they want anyway. You and your father.

Please, Nora, go!"

But as obstinate as he could be, I could match it. "I'm not leaving without you. We can both wait for your family."

"No, it'll be safer for you to go through. Please, just go. I don't want them to hurt you, not after it's my fault they know. I should have known when I saw the business card, but I just couldn't say no when she asked, and I was still so rattled. Look, Nora, do this for me. I don't deserve it, but I need you to be safe."

The pounding on my bedroom door was making my bed quiver. I hesitated, and in that second he pushed me through. I fell through the closet into my room. Before I could get back to the mirror, I could hear the sound of shattering glass. Frantically, I tried to get back to where the noise came from, but all I came up against was the solid wall. I was now stuck in the Thirteenth Realm.

THREE

It had never occurred to me how lacking my education in World Walking was until that moment. Grandmère had explained that only Walkers could exist without throwing off the world as it was meant to be. There were no time altering paradoxes of running into our other selves, as we existed only once. Grandmère had once hinted that some Walkers tried to keep such paradoxes from happening, but other than that, I had no idea what my gift was meant for. And now, without a Portal, it seemed absolutely worthless. I wanted to know that Ivan was safe. He had sacrificed so much, but he had given me up at the same time.

Still at a loss of what I was supposed to do, I got to my feet and wandered around my room. Everything was the same. Except the closet, which, as I had noticed on two occasions, was empty. My bed had the same comforter, the same iron bed frame, my dresser was the same shade of walnut. Even the round braided rug was the same pattern. The pictures I had in my room were missing, as was the bulletin board I had with my art on it.

Other than that, it seemed someone had worked overtime to restore the right feeling. I suppose this might be an example of the Thirteenth Realm folding a space around me. If so, it was doing a fine job. I left my room, wandering down the hall to see if the house itself was the same. I had noticed a few differences the day before, but I wanted to know more. At the top of the stairs, I stopped. Someone was in the house today.

"Peter, is that you?" asked a woman. She turned the corner and I lost my footing. My foot had been poised over the top stair, but at the sight of my dead mother, I crashed down. Rolling down the stairs in painful surprise, I rolled to a stop at her feet.

"Mom?" I asked in muted surprise.

"Nora?" she asked in equal shock. "Your father said you wouldn't be coming until next month." She helped me to my feet and it was then that I realized she was probably six months pregnant. Still, she was my mother. I did what any rational person would do, I hugged her. She laughed uncomfortably and pulled me away. "And to think your father was worried about how you would take a new mother."

"New?" The word stuck in my throat as my brain tried desperately to catch up.

"Well, we're not married yet, but after the baby comes I will be."

"B-b-but..." I trailed off, unable to stop the stutter. Finally, blessedly, my brain caught up with me. If there was more than one Ivan, there had to be more versions of my mother. This woman was still Celeste, but she was not the woman who had given birth to me. I looked at her stomach in something like revulsion. Did that mean she was carrying me? Eww, talk about paradoxes. I mean, same father, sort of the same mother, but the time was off…I just couldn't quite wrap my mind around all the implications. "Where is my dad?" I asked after I could control my tongue.

"He went back to check on you. He said he'd be back in a day or so. But he wanted to make it for your birthday."

My mouth moved, but nothing was coming out. The level of betrayal a girl could experience in one day had to have a stopping point and I was hitting it head on. I couldn't believe what my father had done. Literally, my mind could not wrap around the concept embodied by my own mother, who wasn't actually my mother.

"How long have you been together?" I asked slowly, taking care not to trip over my words.

She frowned slightly, and her hand came to rest on her belly. "He met me about three years ago. We started dating right then." Her expression turned whimsical, and I had to cut her off for fear of hearing more than I bargained for.

"Well, hopefully he c-comes back soon. I need t-t-to talk to him. If you don't mind, I'll g-go out for a moment." Before she could say yay or nay, I was out the door. I was not a natural runner. I was not a natural athlete in any way. My sport of choice was yoga, if that counted as a sport. However, I was in enough shape from mandatory P.E. to struggle through a run. At first I didn't know where I was going, but by the time the breath had been sucked completely from my lungs, I was standing at the park where Ivan and I had once played. Staggering to a picnic table, I collapsed onto it, wheezing and crying. I tried to pinch myself, hoping I would wake from this horrible dream, but despite the pain, I was still stuck here. Reduced to hiccups, I tucked my knees up to my chest and watched a squirrel scurry across the grass and up a tree. The reddish coat glistened like a bright copper penny as he ran across grass the color of emeralds and up a tree that resembled chiseled marble. The colors that had once fascinated me as a child seemed garish now, and I closed my eyes to block out the pain, hiccuping the whole time. Rocking back and forth, I chanted to myself.

"There's no place like home, there's no place like home."

"You need ruby slippers to make that work," said a dry voice behind me. Something about his voice made me shake. It was confusing, even to me, but he sounded like the Ivan from the Twelfth Realm. Slowly, I turned to come face to face with none other than my other Ivan. His lips were compressed in a thin line, and he was watching me like he would a cowering puppy. He met my eyes and his widened in recognition. "It's been awhile," he said in clipped tones.

"I'm so sorry," I whispered around my hiccups. "I t-tried to come back, I left a letter."

He shrugged. "Whatever. What are you doing here anyway?"

I knew from his tone that he had come back to our park before. I had left the letter in one of the tree hollows. Even after five years, he remembered and he must have read the note. He wasn't meeting my eyes. If the Ivan of the Twelfth Realm could read my expressions like an open book, I had similarly learned to read him. However much they might look alike, and be alike, this Ivan wasn't nearly so open, but years of experience came to help me read him now. I took a second to take in how much he had changed. He was dressed in clothes that Ivan of the Twelfth Ream wouldn't have been caught dead in. He had less than couture jeans with a hole on one knee that I had the impression came from wear not style. He wore combat boots and a cable knit shirt with a beanie cap pulled over his long locks. This Ivan wore his hair even longer, and it flipped out from under the cap.

"My father is getting married," I said, my tone broken.

He put his hands in his pockets and rocked back on his heels. "Rough."

"She looks just like my mother," I added, wanting to tell the truth, but knowing now was not the time. "And she's pregnant."

He let out a low whistle. "Poor Princess," he said, sympathy interlaced with mockery. My head snapped up at his tone, and my hiccups were gone in a flash of anger.

"I don't need your pity," I said sharply. Getting to my feet, I stood within inches of him, hating his two inches of height over me.

"Then I won't give it," he replied calmly, his eyes still watching me more intently than was polite. "So, what's the plan, we run around the playground and swing on the swing sets like we did as kids?"

"I don't have a plan," I snapped, secretly happy to have something other than self pity to occupy my thoughts. "I came here because I was miserable. I hardly expected you to be here."

"Didn't you though?" he asked, that mockery evident in his eyes. Before I could find a suitable retort, three boys came up to us. Each was holding a skate board, and they were all dressed similarly to Ivan. Clearly this was a fashion.

"Hey, Ivan, if you're done with your girl-friend," the first boy intentionally forced a pause for affect, "We're heading over to the pipe."

"It's not like I'd get lost," replied Ivan, and I was floored to see his expression. He moved to make sure they couldn't come between us, his eyes flashing at the others in silent challenge. "Besides, we've got to wait for Nick and Cody."

The tallest, a blond with hazel eyes and the only one without a beanie, came up to us. "Aren't you going to introduce us?"

"No."

My poor abused heart beat wildly at his tone. Even after all these years he was still possessive of me. It was a small balm in an otherwise awful day. The blond looked at me, and I was further stunned to see the quick once over of my form left him with a look of appreciation. I blushed to the roots of my blond hair to be so inspected. I had never been viewed as a girl, not like that. Not ever. In a small way it was flattering, but Ivan seemed to take offense to it.

"Go on, Brad, I'll be there before Nick is, anyway." He stepped forward and gave a slight shove to the other boy.

The other two boys wavered, but gave in to the impulse of self preservation and followed the blond. I reached out to touch Ivan's shoulder. He jumped and turned back to glare at me.

"I missed you," I said softly. "I tried to come

back, so many times."

"Then why didn't you?"

"I couldn't get here," I replied.

"You can do anything if you try," he replied, but the one second of true communication between us was gone. His mocking was back in full force. "Come on, Princess, I'll take you home. I can't believe you made it here unscathed. You walked right through Shotgun Corner."

I looked around at the beautiful park in surprise. Nothing looked dangerous. "I ran," I said, letting him lead the way back.

"That might explain it. Look, Princess, this isn't the world you saw before. Your house is probably on the last block of safety. Best you stay on that side."

"What happened?" I asked, staying close to him as we made our way back up. Now that I took the time to look, I could see what he was talking about. While the beauty was more beautiful, it seemed the darkness was now darker. This street had descended in five years from a high end area to broken windows and boarded up doors. Ivan pulled me closer as we passed by a group of people sitting around a stereo. They nodded to Ivan, but their eyes strayed to me.

"Who's your friend?" asked one of the men. Another was busy pounding metal at a makeshift forge. He stopped to stare at me as well. It was disconcerting to say the least. Ivan wrapped his arm around my waist.

"None of your business, Luis." He frowned at the lot of them, but there was no real animosity.

"You coming over for dinner, tonight Ivan?" asked the one who had been working with metal.

"Maybe, depends."

The metal worker nodded. "Yeah, that works. Tell your mom we're making extra tamales. Bring everyone."

Ivan nodded. "I will. Later, Jimmy."

I glanced back over my shoulder as we walked on, surprised that they were all still watching. "Friends of yours?" I asked.

He frowned at me, seeming to just realize his arm was still around my waist. He dropped it as if burned and moved a step further away. "Not friends you need to meet, Princess."

"Why not?" I asked challenging. "Why can't I meet your friends?"

"You going to introduce me to yours?" he asked in return.

I stopped in the middle of the sidewalk, all the fight sapped from me. "You are my only friend," I said so softly he pretended not to hear.

"Sorry?"

I glared, amazed that the tiny spark of anger was still in me. "I left everything behind. Everything. I am here, alone, with no one I know except you. Who am I supposed to introduce you to? My mother, who isn't really my mother? Or my father who never takes the time to care for me? Or my grandmother who I haven't seen in nearly a year? Maybe I want to meet your friends."

He rocked back on his heels, impressed in spite of himself with my display of backbone. A corner of his mouth quirked up, something vaguely like the smile I knew could transform his face. "Alright, ease up. Maybe I'll take you by and let you eat some of Jimmy's mom's home cooking. I doubt you've had the like."

"I doubt it too," I replied, relaxing again. "I usually order Italian."

He startled a half step before falling in line with me. "Well, we'll have to work on that culinary education of yours, Princess." We had made it to the base of the steps up to my house. Celeste was standing there, watching us.

"Nora, what are you doing?" she left unspoken my choice of companion, but Ivan and I both heard the less than flattering implication in her tone.

"This is my friend," I replied tartly, oddly angry with this woman. I shouldn't blame her for my father's actions, but a part of me did, and maybe a smaller part still held my mother guilty for dying. I was never into deep introspection, and it terrified me to even contemplate the darker part of my heart and soul.

"Well, come in, dinner is ready." She frowned at Ivan again and turned back into the house.

"Isn't he invited?" I asked with a bite. Really, this anger was refreshing. It made me brave and combative, two adjectives I would never had used to describe myself before.

Her shoulders tensed, and she turned slowly around. "If you insist, Nora, you can invite your friend."

Ivan's eyes were hooded, but the edge of his mouth was twitching in repressed humor. "I'm good, thank you," he said to Celeste. She nodded curtly and went inside. He reached out and softly touched my arm. "If you want to, I'll come by around eight. Jimmy and his family eat late, his dad doesn't get off until after seven."

I felt my hurt flutter, and I couldn't contain the smile.

"I'd love that."

He nodded, and I liked to think he was satisfied. "See you around, Princess."

I waved, but he didn't turn around to see me. Sighing, I leaned against the railing and watched him. My life had been turned upside down in less time that it took me to watch my favorite movie, but somehow, there was an island of tranquility in my world and that island had always been Ivan. Like feeling a sore tooth, though, I tempered my own happiness with remembrance of how I had come here. It hurt not to know the fate of my other Ivan. It also hurt to know why he was in danger. I couldn't fix anything without help, though. I needed a Portal, and for that I needed to find another Walker. Sighing, I let myself into a house that was so like my own. No one ever said life was easy, I was just having to experience that a little more personally than I might have liked.

FOUR

I had completely forgotten in the last five years what it was like to have a home cooked meal. The extent of my cooking was instant oatmeal. The extent of my father's was scrambled eggs. Was it any wonder I had so many take out numbers memorized? Though, I reasoned, those numbers probably didn't work here. The kitchen had recently been remodeled, and it looked like a beautiful piece straight out of an interior designing catalogue. The counters were white marble with gorgeous silver veins lacing through it. I was no judge, but the glass enclosed cupboards and stainless steel appliances made the room look like a million dollars. I stood in the doorway, almost afraid to step foot on the sparkling tile floor. Celeste turned from the stove and frowned at me.

"Can you put plates out, Nora?"

It was so foreign to do something so simple, that I stood mute for another moment. She heaved a sigh and reached up to get the plates herself. I hurried in, holding out my hands, feeling guilty especially as her apron stretched across her growing belly. My true mother had once raised me to be better.

"Silverware is in the buffet," she said after handing over the china. "Come back for glasses."

It made no sense how I could go from anger to submission in less than five minutes. But then it was so hard to remain harsh with a woman who looked exactly like my mother. When we were seated, she passed the green beans and mashed potatoes, frowning when I put more than a single scoop on my plate.

"So," I said, trying to break the strained silence, "do you know the sex?"

"I beg your pardon?" she asked, quickly putting her napkin to her mouth to cover her cough of surprise.

"The baby," I said, pointing my fork in the general direction of her belly. She frowned again at me. Honestly, she was going to be covered in wrinkles at this rate.

"It's a boy. He's due in January."

"Oh, thank God for miracles then," I said emphatically.

"Nora!"

"What?"

She put her knife and fork down, rubbing her forehead. "I realize you have been living like nothing short of a savage since your mother died, but you could try for some manners."

I grimaced and put my knife and fork down as well. "I used a fork," I muttered, unsettled by her reminder of my mother.

"There is no need to be so crass. Dinner conversations do not usually involve such topics. And please, don't swear."

"I didn't swear," I replied, the odd fission of anger simmering to a near boiling point again. "I could though, my dad taught me all he knows." "Nora," she sighed with enough air to blow out the candles if they had been lit. "I realize this will be difficult for you, but please, try."

I stuffed a roll in my mouth rather than answer that. Difficult did not begin to describe my day. When I reached for more of the potatoes, which were wonderfully seasoned, she tsked.

"What?" I asked, dropping the serving spoon with a painful clatter on the side of the china bowl.

She winced at the noise. "You should really control your serving sizes. I don't mean to sound harsh, but you could really stand to lose a few pounds."

That was all I could take, the straw that broke this camel's back. Throwing my napkin down, I left the room without waiting to be excused. I was nearly eighteen, I should have been more mature, but it hurt to try. I wanted to break something, the anger just rolling through me, but there was nothing that would have satisfyingly shattered in my room.

Celeste did not bother to come and talk me out of my snit. I didn't really blame her. Instead, I was stuck in my room on self inflicted grounding, trying to make sense of what was going on in my world. I stretched through thirty minutes of yoga, hoping it would cool my temper. It might have worked, or prolonged isolation might have done it as well. After flipping through a few magazines that were interesting if only because they were different, I took to twiddling my thumbs and staring at my ceiling. For lack of something better to do, I went back into the closet, desperate but hopeless to find a way back. Not even a shard of my Portal had followed me through.

As I came back out of the closet, I noticed an envelope on the floor. It was the same one from my grandmother that had, albeit indirectly, led to the events of the last twenty four hours. If I had just left it under my bed, if I hadn't pricked my finger on the broken shards, I'd be living in mild dread of a stalker outside my house and an impending birthday. I would not be trying to come to terms with a new Celeste, an old Ivan, and a world that was not my own.

I took the letter with me as I bounced onto my bed, crossing my legs under myself and staring at the rich textured envelope. It didn't look like any sort of paper I had seen before, but then I was largely limited to school notebooks and printer paper. Trying to avoid the cuts on my fingers I had accrued from my Portal, I carefully opened the envelope. As I unfolded the thick paper, I heard a knocking at my window. Nearly jumping off the bed in shock, the letter falling under the bed, I saw Ivan watching me with unveiled amusement. I was on the second story. My brow knit in confusion as to how he was hovering outside my window. It was only when I opened the window that I realized in this house there was a very well established trellis up my side. I had to smile despite everything. Grandmère had once said the worlds held a void that we filled, complete with what we needed most. I apparently needed an alternate way out of my room in this world.

"What are you doing here?" I asked, looking down to fully take in his feat.

"No one answered the door. I figured your future mother didn't appreciate my corrupting influence."

I rolled my eyes. "No, she probably thinks you should have chinos and a sweater. I don't think I've ever eaten a meal on china that wasn't a holiday meal."

He took this all in stride, his wry smile only growing. "So, Princess, you ready for some real food?"

My stomach growled at the thought. Forget Celeste's strictures that I needed to lose weight. I was still in the body mass index range for acceptable weight, I just might be pushing it a bit. "How do I get down?"

"You climb," he replied dryly, but all the same, he helped me come out of the window, staying close enough to help me with my footing. When we landed, he took my hand and led me back down the tiny alley, keeping from any windows on my town house that we could have been seen from.

This time I noticed the changes as we crossed through the neighborhood. Literally, at Merry Avenue, the whole demeanor changed. From pristine and personable town houses, the houses here looked like they had survived the bombardment of World War II. Ivan kept me close as we maneuvered down another street that was similarly abused. The houses looked haunted to me, and I felt them closing in around me the deeper we descended into the rubble. People watched us, keeping their eyes away from me after noticing Ivan. It seemed I was safe with my escort, but I wasn't so confident of what my fate would be alone. After several blocks of what could only be described as a maze, Ivan stopped outside a barred door and rang a door bell. A buzzing sounded from within, and he let us both in. We climbed up four flights of stairs, having to move around two sleeping forms, and I swear I saw a rat.

The guy that had been working with metal on the side of the road earlier opened the door. He saw Ivan and grinned.

"Hey, you made it. Come in, come in." He noticed me and his grin grew bigger. "And you brought company. Well, Mom will be thrilled." He nodded politely to me and shut to door behind us. "Come on, food's through here." Ivan gripped my hand and looked back at me, his expression guarded. I smiled gamely, and some of his dourness lightened. When we entered the dining room, I was amazed at the spread. There were at least a dozen people in the tiny apartment, and the entire table was laid out with enough food to feed an army. The woman behind it all came out with a pot of more food.

"Ivan!" she exclaimed when she saw him. "Here, Luis, take this." She handed the pot into another set of hands and came over to hug Ivan. She looked over at me, and even though she was a good five inches shorter than me, I felt like a delinquent child under her assessing gaze. "You brought company," she said, her words guarded.

"Sofia, this is Nora. Nora, this is Sofia."

Sofia raised her eyebrows, but no answer was forthcoming from my tightlipped companion. "Well, any friend of Ivan's is a friend of ours. Come, my dear, I'll take you through. A first timer can be a bit overwhelmed and these boys are always so bad about sharing." She handed me a plate and took me to the front of the table. I followed along, dutifully adding a little bit of everything. The food was not just Mexican. Yes, there were fresh tamales, they were what had been in the pot, but there was also couscous and, of all things, sushi. Even taking only one of each, I still had double the food Celeste had allowed me at dinner. Sofia took me off to the kitchen while the rest of the party descended like a horde of hungry animals. There were four more women in the kitchen, and two little children in the corner being watched by a boy a few years my junior.

"Jorge, you can go eat now," said Sofia. He took off like a shot, and the other women quickly rearranged matters so that I was safely trapped between them. "So, Nora," said Sofia, "how do you know Ivan?"

I sighed around my first bite of heavenly tamale and set my plate on the table. "We met as kids. I just moved back."

She nodded, glancing to the woman to her right.

"And did he invite you?"

"I hardly invited myself," I replied dryly.

"And how long did you say you've known him?" asked another.

"I didn't," I replied, frowning at this covey of interrogators.

"Leave her be," came another voice from the room leading away from the kitchen. "If Ivan chooses to bring a girl with him, that is his business." She looked at me in consideration. "What is your name my dear?"

"Nora."

Her eyebrows rose to the top of her smooth

olive forehead. I had never met Ivan's mother in this world, but she was unmistakable with her smooth black hair and exotically shaped eyes. This version of Padma Battuta was much wearier, and her hair sported gray streaks that the more coifed version I knew would never have stood for. Her near black eyes took me in, hardly missing a single detail. "Nora," she said, making certain not to leave out anyone in her encompassing gaze, "would you please come with me? Feel free to bring your food with you. Sofia is a master chef."

I was amazed that they all let me up without a single protest. Sofia looked uncomfortable at being caught out. Padma took me through the crowded rooms and out to the tiny balcony. There were no less than five boys squeezed out there, and by the smell of things, they were smoking pot. They saw Padma and ran. One seriously considered bailing over the rails, but was pulled back in by someone else with a degree more of common sense. Padma just waited patiently until they were gone before shutting me out to a new one-on-one form of interrogation.

"I'm sorry about the others," she said softly. "They view Ivan as one of their own. I appreciate it, but that does not mean they should make you uncomfortable."

"I was okay," I said, still too uneasy to start in on my food. She reached across and took the sushi roll.

"Lana's cooking, though I imagine her daughters do most of it these days. You seem to share my opinion on raw foods," she said before taking an experimental nibble. I had chosen the vegetarian version. I put my plate on the rail and we shared my bounty.

"Don't you want some more?" I asked, gesturing inside.

"Oh, no, I know I was too late to make it for anything. Sofia loves her neighborhood dinner nights. Every Wednesday since the shooting," her face grew pensive. "Like clockwork."

"What shooting?" I asked in surprise, but she just shook her head, her long black hair flowing around her shoulders.

"I don't like to talk about it," she said softly. I instantly knew it was personal, and I was afraid of the answer.

"Well, the food is the best I've had in years. I've been ordering pizza for the last five years. It's a nice break."

Her eyes sharpened on me. "No one cooked in your home?"

I laughed and finished my couscous. "Hardly. After my mom died, I had to force my dad to eat at all."

She shook her head more slowly, her expressive face pensive. "If you would like, I could teach you."

"Really?"

"Really."

"I'd like that," I said, meaning every word. For some reason, it seemed right to know now.

"I don't work on Sundays," she said, a wry smile curving up the right side of her mouth. Her gaze flickered to the door. "Does that work for you?"

I shrugged. "Sure. As far as I know, I have no plans, but I'm sure Celeste will come up with something."

"Is that alright with you, Ivan?" she asked the doorway.

I jumped slightly to see that he had joined us. He came out onto the balcony, hunched low with his hands in his pockets.

"Whatever works for you, Mom."

"Then you should bring her over."

"Oh," I interrupted uncomfortably, "Celeste might make me go to church."

"Make you?" asked Padma with polite incredulity.

"Well, I'm sure my father will as well, if he shows up. And since this is all new, I don't want to openly offend anyone."

"Don't worry, I'm sure we can work something out. Can't we Ivan?"

He simply shrugged, watching us both with a guarded expression.

"Thank you," I said awkwardly. "I look forward to it."

Ivan tipped back on his heels as his mother turned to leave. "What about your birthday?"

Padma stopped and turned back. Her eyes flashed first to her son and then fell back to me. "When is your birthday, my dear?"

"It-t-t's Friday." Tears pricked my eyes that Ivan had remembered, but for some reason it suddenly felt like I was put on the spot over something so simple. I couldn't help even such a mild fear from slipping into my speech.

"You should come over after school," said Padma. "Do you have a car?"

I shook my head. I had had a car, I felt like saying, but managed to bite my tongue in time. There was no need to sound like a crazy person to someone who was just trying to be nice.

"Well then," she looked at her son, "you can bring her home with you."

I felt like the world was out of my control, but that was becoming more and more familiar to me.

"What about your family?" asked Ivan, watching me with hooded eyes.

"I don't know," I said honestly. "And it's just my dad and me, but that hasn't been working so well lately," I couldn't keep the bitterness from breaking through. "I wouldn't mind spending time elsewhere, if that's okay with you?"

He shrugged, flicking his gaze back to his mother. "Whatever works for you," he said, but I wasn't positive who it was directed towards. Padma nodded and left us, content with her meddling.

"If you don't want me to come over, just say so," I said, putting the idea out there but hating to hear it agreed on.

He rolled his shoulders, finally pulling his hands from his pockets and going to lean over the railing. "You're fine. Besides, my mom loves to bake. She looks for any opportunity to make a cake. I guess you're doing her a favor." He turned to lean his hips on the metal and watch me. "I can tell you we won't be eating off any fine china."

"Good," I said emphatically. "I've been eating off paper plates for the last five years."

He raised his eyebrows and visibly relaxed. "We'll be taking the bus," he said, still feeling me out. "I sold my car last month."

"I had to leave mine behind," I said tactfully. "Something tells me it'll be awhile before I get another."

He nodded, moving around and finally taking a seat on one of the metal chairs. "Your step mother looks like one of Saguenay's finest."

My brow knit in confusion. The name of the city, it seemed, had changed between worlds. "I should at least give her a chance," I said, taking the other seat. "I mean, it isn't as though I can go back home."

"Burn a few too many bridges?" he asked mockingly.

"Something like that. But besides that, I'm not yet seventeen. I can't legally leave my father."

He gave a half shrug. "Like I said, Princess, you can do whatever you want, you just have to want it enough."

"Not always," I replied sadly. "Sometimes there are just some things you can't get back from."

For the first time all evening, his expression became unguarded. "What would that be?"

"Another world," I said softly.

He leaned back, walls up in an instant. "Sounds like an excuse."

"If I can, I'll show you what I mean," I said.

"If you can?"

"It's complicated," I replied, closing my eyes for a second.

"Life's complicated."

"Tell me about it."

We sat there in something resembling camaraderie. I finally opened my eyes when he shifted, causing the seat to squeak.

"I'm sorry about earlier," he said slowly. "I should have given you a better idea of what was coming."

"Your mom took care of me. And it really

wasn't that bad." I paused, and he didn't offer anything more. "Do I get to meet your friends?"

"I'll invite them on Friday," he replied with humor.

"Are they already gone?" I asked, looking back into the apartment.

"Most of them. Their moms showed up to take them home. It is a school night." His face twisted in a grimace. "Which reminds me that I should be getting you back." He smoothly slid to his feet, and after a second thought, he held out his hand to help me to mine. Slightly surprised, I took the offered help.

"School?" I asked in some concern.

"Yeah. Despite the demarcation line, you're in the East Ward, you'll be going to Golden Gate Academy, just like the rest of us."

"Academy?"

He smiled, but there was no humor in his eyes. "You're from the right side of Shotgun Avenue, Princess, you'll be fine. Come on, even with me, it'll be a rough trip back." He didn't let go of my hand, pulling me out of the apartment with little more than a wave to everyone who was still there. He was right, over half of the numbers had disappeared, especially anyone our age.

There was something to be said for having his escort on the way back. The dark alleys that had seemed in the twilight to be closing in on me were downright suffocating on the way back. Some intrepid souls still lived in the upper stories of the ruined houses, but fires and candles had been substituted for power. Not even street lamps worked down here. It was a full two blocks before the first street light flickered on above us. Ivan had yet to let go of me, and I moved still closer as I saw the faces looking back at us from the shadows. We didn't say a word to each other until we had crossed back to the street I now lived on. I let out the breath I didn't realize I had been holding, and he released my hand. We slipped back down the alley and he helped me start up the trellis. I tumbled through the open window, feeling bruises that had formed in the last day before grow larger. He slipped in after me, and got me to my feet before unceremoniously pushing me onto the bed.

"Don't try and come back on your own," he said in warning.

I opened my mouth to protest, but his demand was a very good one and when it came right down to it, I couldn't argue.

"Thanks for taking me," I said honestly. "It was wonderful."

"You need to get out more, Princess." He started to climb back out, pausing half way out the window sill. "Just not don't go out past Shotgun Avenue."

"I got that warning the first time," I said wryly. "I can listen."

He shrugged and slipped the rest of his body through smoothly. Peeking his head back, he smiled at me. "You weren't all that good at it before." He tapped his chin and pointed at me. "Remember that? Like I said, see you around, Nora."

I rubbed my scar absently. He had told me not to climb the monkey bars, I had ignored him only to be stung by a wasp and fallen off in shock, splitting my chin and knocking out two baby teeth. Grandmère had found us shortly after and taken me to a hospital, Ivan in tow. I sighed and collapsed on the bed, suddenly exhausted beyond words. I didn't even manage to take my shoes off before falling asleep. It had been a very trying day, and that was the understatement of my lifetime.

FIVE

For some unknown reason, the alarm on my nightstand went off at six thirty the next morning. Groaning, I opened one eye to look at it and groaned again. Heaving myself out of bed, I blindly wandered off in the direction of my bathroom. When I turned the lights on, my mind was instantly jolted awake. This was not my bathroom. It had been remodeled in the same theme as the kitchen. Black and white was the color scheme, with black granite counter on two pedestal sinks. I blinked at my reflection in the gilded mirror. The starkness of the colors made me look like a zombie. I felt like a zombie. Edging towards the shower, oddly apprehensive of what I would find on the other side, I pulled the glass door open only to find more shiny surfaces. There was a bottle of shampoo and conditioner. Squinting, I pulled one towards me, surprised that it was my brand. Edging back slowly, I started the water and shut the door while I waited for the water to warm. The gilded mirrors turned out to be cabinets inset in the wall. Opening one, I found hair products I could use. I took a black towel towards the shower with me and hurried through in the fastest shower I had ever taken. Everything felt wrong, like I was using something that wasn't mine. Who was I fooling? It wasn't. I was dressed in record time, but I was also slightly disturbed to find that I had to wear the same clothes as I had the day before. My dresser drawers were empty. Wet hair still hanging down my back, I trotted down for a Pop Tart. I walked into the kitchen and came face to face with evidence that my world had turned on its axis.

Celeste turned around and shrieked.

"Nora, what are you doing?"

"Looking for breakfast?"

"You need to be leaving in ten minutes for school! Where is your uniform?"

"Uniform?"

She heaved a sigh and stepped away from the stove, pulling the kettle off just as it began to whistle. "I told Peter this would happen. I guess today is a shopping day. I'll call the school to tell them you won't be in until tomorrow." She looked me over and found me wanting. "Is that all you have?"

"Yes," I replied, frustration pushing me to drag out the word.

She sighed again. "Well, sit down and have some fruit. Would you like a cup of tea?"

"Do you have any Pop Tarts?"

She nearly spilled her tea. The steaming beverage slopped over the pristine counters and she busied herself with cleaning the mess before answering. "Nora, I realize you and your father lived a very different life, but while you are in my house you will be eating balanced meals."

It rankled to hear her refer to my house. I had to force breath in past my anger and tell myself *this* was not my house. That had been left behind. With a sigh, I took a banana and began to peel it very slowly, watching her carefully. "Just out of curiosity," I asked bitingly, "what is it you thought I did while my dad was living here with you?"

She set her cup down with infinite care and faced me. "You were with your grandmother, of course."

"Hardly," I said snorting and taking a bit of banana. "Deep down, I might appreciate your stance that we work things out, but let's get something very clear. He left me alone to come live with you. End of story, so when you get all high and mighty, it was not me and my dad roughing it, it was me surviving as a teenager would."

Her blue eyes widened, and I saw something like the tenderness I had once seen in my mother's eyes shine out. It made a lump form in my throat.

"Alright, then," she said in a much more gentle tone, "let's start at the beginning. Do you like coffee?" she asked.

I nodded distractedly, wondering where this was going.

"We'll stop for a cup on our way to get you some clothes. If you're ready?"

"Sure." I slid off the bar stool. It seemed only right to meet her half way. "Where does this go?" I asked about the banana peel.

"Here," she took it and put it in a little canister. "Compost. I'm trying a flower box off my window." She smiled, a little unsure of our standing, but seeing me for a near adult for the first time. "Do you grow any plants?"

I laughed wryly and shook my head. "Hardly. When my mom died, my dad threw all her plants away."

She sighed and shook her head. "Sometimes I think Peter sabotages my attempts to grow even a cactus. I guess that makes sense if she grew things."

I frowned and waited for her to put a jacket on. "You shouldn't let him win. I'll help you grow them. He's not likely to come into my room to kill them."

Her mouth curved into an "o". "That would be…nice. Thank you, Nora."

I shrugged, still struggling with how to work with her. "Don't mention it. Are we going?"

"Of course."

We rode in awkward silence. I couldn't come up with where to start. I had to constantly remind myself this woman was a stranger. I wanted to just jump in and tell her about the last five years of my life, how hard it had been living with my dad, but she wouldn't understand. She might empathize, but she wouldn't be able to sympathize. We sat down for our coffee, and I was pleased that she let me have a scone and a latte without a word about my weight.

"So, what do you do in your free time?" she asked politely.

"I like to take pictures, but I had to leave my cameras behind."

"Well, your birthday is coming up soon, isn't it? We'll look for one today for you."

"You don't have to," I said uncomfortably.

"Don't be silly, Nora. You're going to be my

daughter soon, I would do no less for a child of mine." Her hand absently touched her growing belly, and I felt a sliver of jealously. It made me wonder how my mother had felt about me.

"Well, thanks," I said in the ensuing silence.

"Of course, are you done?"

"Yeah."

"Good, shall we?" She rose and waited for me. "We shouldn't make this a habit. Rather a treat for good behavior."

And just like that the good will vanished. She noticed and hastened to add.

"Of course I can't drink any coffee, but I'm always so tempted, and the smell of it makes me want to cry from wanting."

She hadn't backtracked the insinuation, but I had to take a deep breath and let it slide. Besides, she might have a point. I had yet to see a single person who didn't look like they walked off a movie set. This world didn't seem to have an obesity problem. Maybe Ivan or Padma could answer that for me. I wasn't about to ask the woman beside me.

We made it to the first shop that she had written down, and a shop clerk took us back to the uniform section.

"Do you have larger sizes?" asked Celeste, pitching her voice in what she had to hope was low enough for me not to hear.

The shop clerk glanced at me. "We should. Most of the smaller sizes sell out before school starts. We should be fine with something for her."

I seethed, and deep breathing didn't help. Where oh where had the shy and retiring Nora gone? "I'm standing right here," I said through clenched teeth. "And I think I can find my own damn size."

"Nora!" Celeste looked apologetically at the clerk.

"Does no one swear around here?" I asked bitingly. "Do you want me to educate you all?"

"Absolutely not! Please, go look for a skirt. You'll need at least two, and then we can try jackets."

"Right." I stalked off to the skirts, and, sure enough, there were far more 10s than 4s or 6s. I pulled off one and went back to try it on while Celeste apologized for my behavior. I felt no need to offer an apology. Honestly, I was supposed to appreciate the derogatory terms about my body? I liked the way I was, at least I had no urges to stick my finger down my throat. They could deal with it.

Everyone's feathers were smoothed an hour later when we left with my entire year's worth of mandatory clothes. After that came shopping for something that wasn't gray and white and striped all over. We had lunch, in which I was careful to order a salad, before Celeste took me to a camera store. I nearly forgot every negative feeling I had about her as she let me have my way for half an hour.

It sounds horrible to say, but my father had never done this. He had bought me things, but preferred to leave me with one of his credit cards. When I was younger, he and my mom had always taken me out on my birthday and given me a budget to spend, but if I really wanted something as a child, I had told my grandmother. She alone had taken me shopping on rainy days. She and

Twelfth Ivan were the only ones who knew of my passion for photography. Now, to top off all sort of surprises, it seemed this Celeste had more than a passing fancy for the art as well. She helped me pick out my Olympus, and she didn't even blink at the price.

"You know, Nora," she said as we made our way back to her BMW, "we could turn the basement into a dark room. I always wanted to develop my own pictures, but I'm sure you prefer to do it all on a computer."

"No," I said, shocked nearly speechless, "I like developing pictures. I prefer black and whites. They just seem better when I do it myself. There was a dark room at my school."

She nodded, letting us in and waiting while I stuffed my most recent purchase in with everything else. "Funny how some things don't go out of fashion," she said with a small smile. "We'll have to ask your father about doing that."

I frowned, my enthusiasm instantly drained. "You'll have to ask," I said, sulking down in my seat. "If you see him."

She watched me uneasily, but didn't say anything more. We went back home much as we had left, in total silence. I felt uncomfortable asking her to help me move everything upstairs. I had never been around a pregnant woman before. I didn't know what to expect or what was too much, and she didn't argue. It took four trips there and back and when I was done, I collapsed on my bed in desperate need of a breather. I must have dozed off after a chaotic day of shopping, because it was early evening when I heard voices downstairs. Blinking back sleep from my eyes, I went down to investigate. Everything hurt as I stretched going down the stairs. My running around and falling down the stairs had hurt everything I could name. Cricking my neck, I came to a halt two steps from the entry hall as I recognized the other voice. My father was here.

"What do you mean she's here?" he was near shouting.

"What I said," Celeste replied. I was further surprised to hear her voice starting to crack. "She showed up yesterday."

"But why didn't she go back home?"

"Why don't you ask her? She is your daughter."

"Damn it, Celeste, this wasn't supposed to happen."

"That isn't my fault!"

"Are you crying?"

"Of course I'm crying! You're yelling at me for reasons outside my control!"

"You could have sent her home!"

"Hardly, I don't know where she comes from. I don't even know where you come from!" I stood in stupefied immobility and my location was a hazardous one as Celeste came hurrying around the corner. She saw me and the tears that were welling in her blue eyes spilled over and she went up the stairs sobbing. I turned from that surprise to come face to face with my father. My skin rippled in an angry convulsion.

"Dad," I said sharply.

"Nora, what are you doing here?"

"I could ask you the same thing," I replied, crossing my arms across my chest.

"Don't get smart with me Alinora. How did

you find a Portal? Why didn't you go back where you belong?"

My body had progressed to a full out shudder of repressed rage. I had discovered in the last few hours that if I was angry, I could control my stutter, but I lost that control when I was furious or terrified. "Don't you want to know how I'm doing?" I asked, feeling my control begin to slip. "I'm f-fine, b-b-by the way. Even t-though someone t-tried to attack Ivan and b-b-broke into my home!"

He didn't even pause to notice my discomfort. "You should have stayed there. You weren't supposed to come here, not yet. I had a plan."

"Well, it s-sucked!" Pushing past him, I ran out the front door. I didn't make it very far before sitting down and crying in frustration. I really had to come up with a better outlet for all this anger. I hiccuped for a good five minutes before regaining enough composure to head back home. I really didn't want to go back, but I didn't see what options I had.

SIX

Luckily for me, Ivan had shown me how to get in without directly seeing my father, and so I climbed up my trellis and curled up on my bed for another miserable five minutes of self pity. As I lay there, I noticed the envelope from my grandmother that I had forgotten about the day before. Falling gracefully from the bed, I crouched beside it and finally opened the letter.

My Dearest Nora,

> *I won't be able to see you on your birthday. I've been quite busy World Walking. I'm afraid this is my best chance to send a letter to you. If you read this, try not to panic. Ask your father to come for me. He'll know how to get here. If not, you can try World Walking through your broken Portal. You're a Walker, my dear, and your blood is what is needed to cross. Don't go all melodramatic, a drop or two will do. No matter how it goes, please make sure someone comes. I hate to ask for any sort of help, but I fear this is beyond me.*
>
> *Your Loving Grandmère*

Besides the obvious, this was unsettling. My grandmother was quite right, she never asked for help. However, as I was now stranded in this world, I had no idea what to do. I looked over the letter, the only clue I could find was in the envelope itself. A fragment of another Portal had been included, about the size of an old fifty cent piece. It had half of its maker's mark on it, and one number. Grandmère had once explained the marks on my Portal. It was made by Ignacio de Terre, my great-great-great-great-great grandfather. It had also been numbered for what realm it was meant. The one number remaining on Grandmère's shard was a three. I shivered slightly. No realm in the thirties had been safe to cross into when I was younger. They were either at war in a modern age or stuck in war in a barbaric one.

My stomach roiled at the thought of finding my father and explaining this to him, but I couldn't see that I had too many options. Heaving a sigh, I got to my feet and went out to find him. He wasn't upstairs, so I trotted down to the bottom. He wasn't in the living room or the kitchen. Confused, I trotted back up, having to stoop to listening at doors for any sounds of life. I finally found the sniffles of Celeste and knocked at that door.

"Yes?"

I cautiously opened it a crack to find her curled up in the fetal position on the master bed, or as curled up as a six month pregnant woman could be. "Celeste?"

"What is it Nora?"'

I crept half a step in. "Do you know where my dad went?"

She shook her head and rolled away from me.

"No, and right now I don't care."

Sighing, I shut her back in her self pity. It seemed popular media liked to paint pregnant women as highly emotional. I guess it was true. I went back down to the kitchen, needing to eat something after all my shopping and a mere salad. Sadly, Celeste stocked only healthy food. I settled for an apple. It seemed that my father did what he does best when faced with conflict, he too had run. I wandered outside, making it all the way to the dividing line between my neighborhood and Ivan's. It was growing darker, twilight was coming earlier every day. I sat down on the street corner and watched the cars go by. Someone across the street stopped at the sight of me and jogged across the street.

"Nora?"

I looked up at Jimmy. "Hey," I replied dejectedly, taking another bite of my apple.

"What are you doing down here, *chica*?"

I shrugged and got to my feet, dusting off my jeans. "It seemed like something to do."

"You're really close to the battle line," he said, glancing around, and I noticed how trained the motion was.

"What happened here?" I asked.

His face turned into a mask. "It was nasty, come on, let me get you something to drink. Up the block is a little coffee joint that is safe."

"You don't have to," I argued, letting him led me along all the same.

"I think it is."

He didn't say another word or let me say anything until we were seated with our coffee at the Coffee Bean. Starbucks I was used to, and

Starbucks this was not, but it still had a cozy atmosphere, even if the wallpaper was peeling in places. They also served desserts, and their sign made a claim about their pie. It must have been half way decent for in the midst of getting me a hot chocolate, Jimmy got a slice of lemon meringue. The waitress winked at him, and gave him thirty percent off. When we were seated, he finally nodded to me.

"Okay, you can ask. This place is safe enough for those sort of questions."

"Clearly," I said dryly, looking pointedly at the waitress as she brought us our drinks and his pie. I also noticed she had only brought one fork.

He was three bites in before he bothered to stop. "Aren't you going to ask?"

"Can you eat and answer at the same time?"

He smiled at me and finished eating. "I can try."

"Alright, what happened to create Shotgun Alley?"

"It was about five years ago, the Mayor came down for the annual Thanksgiving parade. Someone had holed up in one of the upper stories off Current Street near the intersection with Merry Avenue and fired one shot. It killed him instantly. The Deputy Mayor, well, he didn't take that too well. He cracked down, but no one knew who the shooter was." Jimmy paused, contemplating his pie with a melancholy expression. "I should have asked, do you want any?"

"No, I'm good. You were saying?"

"Well, it pissed the old boy off. He started taking random people in and interrogating them. He finally got Gary Turnpike to crack, or at least that's what he said. Everyone around here knew he was giving a name to save his own skin. And everyone knew how much Dayle Elliot hated Lenin. It was only a matter of time before he got what he wanted out of someone."

"Wait, who is Gary? Dayle? Lenin?"

He sighed and took a sip of coffee, dessert gone. "I forgot. Ivan said you were new to town. You must have lived in another country to have missed the headlines. We were national news for months. Gary Turnpike, he used to work nights at the power plant. He was no one, just a scapegoat. Dayle Elliot is now the mayor, and Lenin, Lenin was Ivan's father."

"Oh. My. God." A few pieces fell into place, and I felt foolish for not putting some together myself. I had only known Twelfth Ivan's father as Len or Mr. Battuta.

He nodded, taking another sip of his Colombian Drip. "It was a nasty time all around. There was, of course, nothing to pin the murder on Lenin, he was framed and we all knew it. I think Elliot knew it too, but he had hated Lenin for years. Rumor has it they both liked Padma at school and she chose Lenin. Anyway, Lenin went into hiding, we all took turns keeping him safe, but it drove Elliot mad. He issued marshal law on anything past Merry Avenue. He even had the Governor give him access to the National Guard. It was brutal. There was nothing left for Lenin to do but turn himself in for a crime he didn't commit, but at the last minute, someone came in and got him out of the state. Not even Padma knew who she was or where she took him. However, he had made a public appearance stating his intentions. Even the

Governor wouldn't let the bombardments continue when Elliot's own men lost Lenin. You've seen the aftermath."

"How long did this go on?"

"At least six months. It was horrible, and ran through the winter. Not that we have the worst winters, but they become a lot harsher when you have no electricity. Elliot's never turned the power back on full time. We get it during the day, but after dark, we're still held on lock down."

"Why don't you move?"

He laughed and shook his head. "He wouldn't let us. Downtown there is a database with every person who has ever lived in the Third Ward. We're on a watch list. In his mind, we're all accomplices. Hell, he locked up Padma on some b.s. charge for six months."

"What about Ivan?"

"He took care of his brothers, and we took care of him. You know the phrase it takes a village?" I nodded. "Well, when we all took over for Padma while she was locked away, we considered ourselves a village raising those three kids. Each one is like another son or brother to all of us. It's why my mom took such an interest in you. You're the first person Ivan's ever brought from outside the border."

"Thank you," I said at last. "For telling me."

He smiled at me. "I figured no one else would. Ivan won't talk about it, and I don't blame him, and if you get from anyone outside Shotgun Alley, you're bound to get the new Mayor's spin of it."

I nodded in agreement, still dazed by the impact of what he had just divulged. "You said this was five years ago?"

"Give or take."

I closed my eyes, overwhelmed by what that meant. At the same time I had been separated from this realm, Ivan had needed me most.

"What's wrong?"

I shook my head to clear my threatening tears. "I couldn't come back five years ago. My father kept me at home, and I didn't make it back until yesterday."

He whistled through his teeth. "I remember. We all wanted to meet you. For years, but Ivan never let us. Then you weren't there. He never said a word. If there's one thing to know about Ivan, it's that if he won't give you an answer the first time you ask, it's best not to ask again."

Trying to break the mood, I smiled wryly at him. "And I'm sure you found that out the hard way?"

He nodded, taking my cue and smiling in return. "The first time I tried, personally, was the first time I saw you. He nearly beat me to a pulp for asking, and he is not only smaller and scrawnier than I am, he's two years younger. None of the other boys dared try after they saw what happened to me."

"Does that mean you're done with school?"

"Yeah, graduated last year. My advice to you, stay low and don't bring too much attention to yourself."

"And you learned that from experience?"

"That too." He laughed with me. Several others that had been at his mother's feeding frenzy were filtering in. They saw Jimmy and came to sit with us.

"So," said the biggest, the man I knew as Luis,

"this is Ivan's little friend. Nice to finally meet you, I'm Luis."

I shook his hand, seeing mine dwarfed by his. He was massive and intimidating. "I'm Nora."

"It's been a long time coming, *chica*."

"And serves Ivan right," replied another, pulling a seat over backwards to join our table. There were at least seven people, three girls around my age and four guys, Luis was the oldest. A few more came over just to pat Jimmy on the back. The rest ran through introductions but I was too overwhelmed to keep track. They all talked to me, but they scarcely let me get a word in edgewise. That was fine, honestly. So many people tended to make me stutter in apprehension. Jimmy, noticing my growing discomfort, finally pulled me free.

"I'm sure Nora will be missed soon, and we don't want the cops coming down," he said, helping me to the door. "See you around."

I waved at everyone before following him outside.

"Thanks."

"Don't do crowds, do you?"

"No, not really."

"Hey, I understand. And you're going to be one of the hottest topics in our world for awhile. Poor Ivan, I know why he doesn't bring anyone into our world, but he really should have saved you the notoriety."

We marched up the streets in companionable silence. "So," he said when we could see my house, "what brought you down to our end, anyway?"

I sighed, and felt around in my back pocket, pulling out my grandmother's envelope. "I wanted to ask my dad about this, but he ran when my future step mom and I confronted him with his lack of planning."

Jimmy pulled out the paper, and the mirror shard nearly fell to the ground but I managed to snag it, crying out when the glass cut me yet again. I was afraid of what would happen with my blood on it and quickly wiped it clean.

"Do you mind?" he asked, taking the shard from me.

I handed it over, silently praying no light show would accompany it. "I could make a covering, turn it into a necklace if you'd like," he said, turning it over carefully. He held it up to his eye to stare at the maker's mark. "I've seen this somewhere," he said more to himself than to me.

"Really?" I asked in building excitement.

"Yeah, I just don't know where."

I took the shard back and looked at the mark myself. "I could make a copy really quick. If you don't mind, I'd like to keep this until I have a chance to talk to my dad."

"Sure, I could ask around about the mark. When you're ready, I could make something to protect the edges. Does it mean something?"

I nodded. "I just don't know what." Glancing up at my house, I sighed. "Come on, no offense, but it's best if I don't take you in through the front."

"None taken," he replied, following as I led him around the side to the base of my trellis. Lucky for me the other bedrooms faced the front of the street. I was slightly surprised that he didn't follow, but it took me only a few quick strokes to get a good sketch of everything on the shard. Folding it up, I carefully climbed back down. When I landed, I was surprised to see Jimmy had company. Ivan was watching me with those hooded eyes that made me nervous.

"Hey Ivan," I said awkwardly. Pulling the paper out of my back pocket, I handed it over to Jimmy, but he didn't take it, instead watching Ivan.

"You weren't at school," Ivan said, striving to keep any emotion from his voice, but Jimmy started to hum in a failed attempt to lighten the mood.

"No, seems you need uniforms. Celeste took me shopping all day. Sadly, I think I'll be there tomorrow."

He nodded, but he didn't leave. Instead, he transferred his direct gaze to his friend. "And what are you doing in this end of town?"

Jimmy shrugged good naturedly. "She wanted me to look into something. Have a problem with that?"

"What?"

I handed the paper instead to Ivan, as Jimmy had never taken it from me. "It's a maker's mark on a piece of mirror from my grandmother."

Ivan took the paper and stared at it for a few long moments. "I've seen this," he said quietly.

"Yeah, me too, I just don't know where," said Jimmy.

"Why do you need to know where it comes from?" Ivan asked me sharply.

I frowned right back at him. "I need to find where my grandmother got it. Theoretically, I could find her."

"You know there are professionals to do this sort of thing," he said sarcastically.

"Maybe, but I highly doubt they'd believe me if

I told them what I was looking for." Both boys raised their eyebrows in surprise.

"Care to elaborate?" asked Ivan.

"Not really. I need to talk to my dad about this, but he's hardly ever available. I thought it best if I had more than one person to help out."

Both of them frowned at me, in near identical expressions of doubt, but I didn't really care. I was not about to explain to them about my World Walking grandmother or why I was stuck here looking for her. That sort of conversation took trust, and I wasn't quite ready to try that worthless trust exercise of closing my eyes and falling backwards and hoping someone caught me.

"Well, I'll look into this Nora." Jimmy took the paper from Ivan and folded it up. "I take it that is the best way to get a hold of you?" he asked, nodding towards my window.

"It seems that way," I replied.

"See you around then." He gave one last speculative glance towards Ivan before turning back towards his home.

I was left staring at Ivan. He was watching me with the same sort of scrutiny, but neither of us were talking.

"Do you want to come in?" I asked, gesturing towards the house.

"Probably best if I didn't," he replied. "Your step mom didn't seem too thrilled with me yesterday."

A wild notion ran through my mind, and I had to contain the crazy laugh that followed. He rocked back and watched me with anticipation.

"Would you be willing to do me a favor?" I asked.

"Depends," he replied slowly.

I started to circle around him, taking in his appearance. I leaned down and untucked his pants from his boots, brushing out the wrinkles before getting back up. I pulled his hat off, secretly impressed he had ditched his mandatory uniform so quickly. Smoothing his long hair from where I had disrupted it, I also pulled off his jacket and straightened his shirt.

"What on earth are you doing?" he asked, all the same not moving.

I took his bag and jacket and put it at the base of the trellis. "I need your help. If my dad's home, this'll work."

"What will work?"

"You look just like a friend I had, and it might just startle him enough to pay attention to me." I stopped from pulling him around the alley, as I had no keys to the back door and having tried it earlier, knew it to be locked. He bumped into me at my sudden stop. "Ivan," I said, "do you remember what I told you about where I come from in the letter I wrote?"

He didn't bother to deny receiving the letter this time. "It didn't make a whole lot of sense, Princess. Kind of like you right now."

"I need you to trust me for fifteen minutes max."

"I don't even know you."

"You did."

"And I trusted her. You're not the same."

"I am," I replied earnestly. "And somewhere, despite everything, so are you."

"People change, Nora."

"Yes, but not us, not really." I took his hand in

mine, looking down at it, hoping for a way to get through to him. "You've been my best friend my entire life. If you want, I'll tell you my deepest secret, but I need you to trust me first."

Something flickered deep in his soul, glimmering on the surface. "Okay, I'll play along, but someday you'll explain this, right?"

"Absolutely."

"Then lead on, Princess."

I kept his hand in mine as we made our way around to the front. Letting us in was easy, but I stopped him after we entered and listened hard. I could hear voices upstairs and I let out a small sigh. My father was home.

"Do you want something to eat? I warn you, though, Celeste doesn't have much in the way of snacks. Unless you like fruit, dried or fresh."

He followed me along to the kitchen, head rotating to take in the remodeled splendor. "I'm good."

"Water? Please, take something."

"Water sounds perfect. What is this about?"

"Shh," I stopped when I heard the voices stop. Then a door opened. I hurried to pull Ivan along, depositing him at the kitchen bar and plopping a bottle of water down in front of him. I took a swig of my own and nearly choked on it as my father came inside.

"Nora, what is going on? Who is this?"

Narrowing my eyes, I gave a tiny nod to Ivan. "Don't you recognize him, Dad?"

Ivan turned to face my father, and my father could have been knocked over with a feather.

"What have you done, Nora?" he asked in a strangled whisper.

"Not a thing, Dad."

"You brought him with you?"

"No, he brought himself."

"What were you thinking? Do you have any idea what would happen if he ran into himself here?"

"What, you mean something like meeting Mom?"

He turned the color of a ripe tomato. "This is not a game, Alinora."

"No," I replied, leaning nonchalantly against the counter. "I have to agree with you. But you don't seem to consider that this door swings both ways."

"You have to take him back, and you have to stay with him."

"Really?" I asked with false surprise. "You want me to go live in Shotgun Alley?"

"What? No, you need to go back to Santa Rosa."

I smiled, but if I had to come up with an adjective, I would say it was evil. "No can do, but if you want me to go home with Ivan, I'm sure he could make sure we weren't robbed on the way to his house, right Ivan?"

He was watching me closely, and I was pretty certain that with only a few more words, he would be close to a pretty accurate answer. His sharp brain was working overtime. "Sure, but we'd have to leave pretty quick. Lights go out in half an hour."

My father's head swung between the two of us faster than a spectator at a tennis match. "He's from this Realm?"

"Yes, if you had bothered to listen to me when

you got here, you'd know that," I snapped.

"But you nearly told him everything."

"Hardly, you might have, but don't worry, I intend to explain it all anyway."

"You can't, Nora." My father came around to grab a hold of my arm again. His bruises were still fresh and I winced. Ivan leaned across the counter and pulled my father back. My father tried to shake him off, still glaring at the both of us. "He's a Seer, he can't know what we are."

"A what?" I asked in confusion. Ivan hadn't let go, and he gave a sharp tug. My father furiously pulled away.

"Didn't my mother tell you anything?"

"Obviously not."

"Now is not the time or the place," he replied sharply, looking pointedly at Ivan.

"It is never the time or the place," I said bitterly. "If I let you go now, I'll never get an answer out of you." I pulled the letter from my pocket and thrust it at him. "While we're at it, what do we do about this?"

He read through and Ivan finally sat back down. "Damn. Look, can you care of Celeste for a day or so?"

"You mean like I've been taking care of myself for the last five years?"

He frowned, but was too distracted to answer with any heat. "She's very sensitive right now, and with the baby coming."

"About that," I spit out, anger flaring in full flame, "w-when w-were you going to tell me? And d-do you realize that if not for a wonderful miracle of probability, that could be me?"

He jumped as if I had stung him, the paper

fluttering to the counter. "I always meant to tell you."

"You just never did."

"The time was never right."

"You should have made the time right! I had a r-r-r-" I took a breath and regrouped. "I had a right to know!"

He sighed, looking down at the letter but not picking it up. "Yes, you did, and I'm sorry about that. But now that you're here, we'll try and make a go of it."

"Try and make a go of it? What if I want to go back? Did you ever think to ask me anything?" Unbeknownst to me, Ivan had picked up the letter and was reading its incriminating words. "How would I get back anyway?"

My father sighed and ran a hand through his hair. "Now's not a good time, Nora. There are Seers out for me, and for you now too. Look, I'll explain it all when I get back, but right now, I need to see some people about your grandmother. Take care of Celeste for me."

Before my astonished eyes, he left then. I slid to the floor, too drained to cry, but wanting so badly to do nothing else.

"Nora, what does this mean?"

I had forgotten for a moment about Ivan. Looking up over my shoulder, I felt my stomach plummet as he held up the letter.

"You remember that secret I told you about?" I asked.

"Yeah, this is it? What is a World Walker?"

"I can't really show you right now. I don't have a Portal."

"You're crazy," he said, getting up quickly and

heading for the door. I dashed after him.

"Ivan, wait!" I managed to dive and grab hold of his arm before he made it out the door.

"What?"

I thought wildly for something to keep him. Finally, I pulled the mirror shard from my pocket. This time, I could only hope for a different outcome than with Jimmy. "Wait just a second more," I begged. Taking the sharpest end, I pricked my finger. My blood ran down the sides, and just as he was turning to leave me, no doubt for good, the mirror began to ripple and flicker, lights flashing around the entry hall. The molten liquid in my hands burned, and I dropped it. He reached out and caught it. The second it touched his hand, it stopped moving.

"How did you do that?" he asked softly.

"It's hard to explain," I said. "If I had a Portal, it would be so easy, but mine broke, it's why I'm stuck here."

"So you're what? Some sort of time traveler?"

"Not really." I took his hand that held the mirror. A drop of my blood touched it again, and, steadied by his hand, the fragment didn't melt this time. Instead, it showed some sort of slide show through a world not our own. It looked like something out of the nightmares of the hobbits in the *Lord of the Rings*. Pleasant village after village was being ravished by brutal industry. The people that flashed across were dressed in bygone fashions. There was little doubt that we were either watching a tiny movie reel or we were seeing another world. Ivan pulled our hands closer, greedily taking in the sights that flashed across.

"Is this what you meant when you said you

came from another world and you had to go back to it?"

"Yes."

"And when you said even your other Ivan would never replace me?"

I sighed. "Do you believe enough to listen?"

"I don't see any other options," he replied, but the mocking emptiness was gone. A trace of the boy I had known was showing through.

"Come on," I pulled him upstairs. I dutifully checked on Celeste, but she had fallen asleep and was softly snoring. Going back to my room, I shut the door behind us. He had taken a seat on the bed and sat watching me. I stayed standing, pacing in agitation. Oddly enough, around him, I didn't feel my tongue try and glue itself to the roof of my mouth.

"I don't know how to make you believe me without showing you another world, but just try to hear me out, okay?" he nodded, leaning back against the bed frame. "When I was six, my grandmother gave me my first portal. That day was the day I met you. I came back all the time, whenever I could. Even after I found other worlds, I even found you in them, this was always the one realm besides my own that I came back to."

"I exist in other realms?"

"Of course. Everyone does, except me and others like me. My future step mother down the hall? In my world she was my mother."

He grimaced and shook his head, trying to grasp what I was telling him. I didn't blame him. It was hard for me, and I had grown up knowing about my heritage.

"In my world, my best friend was you, but not

you. He was that world's version. However, it wasn't the same. You were always my favorite." He curled his lip.

"I'm not sure I like the idea that you wandered around sampling versions of me."

"What else was I to do? My parents always loved each other first and then thought of me second. My grandmother was always busy in some other world. All I had were the friends I met in my world and others worlds. When I was twelve, my mother died. I tried to find you afterwards, but you were gone. I left that note, but when I came back my father broke my Portal. I've been stuck in my world since, until I cut my finger on an edge. It re-formed enough, and I brought that Ivan through. It was a mistake."

He raised an eyebrow mockingly. "Really? How so?"

I sighed, and sat on the chair beside my desk. "You said you'd listen."

"No offense, Princess, but do you hear the words coming out of your mouth?"

"Do you think I don't know how crazy they sound? But it's the truth. However, yesterday, no, the day before? It's been chaos, anyway these men came for my father, and I guess me. That Ivan had given away what I was, and they followed him. He broke the Portal after I passed to protect me. It is why I'm here and why I can't go back."

He didn't immediately say anything, and I had to hope that was a good thing. "If you were anyone else, I'd call mental health services," he said at last. "But I tried to follow you a couple times. I saw you disappear into thin air. I thought," he stopped himself with a violent shake of his head.

"Never mind. This makes more sense, I guess, in retrospect. So, how do you get back to your world?"

His tone was altered, I felt a flutter of hope. "I don't. First off, I have no Portal, no way to get there, and second, I don't know if I'd be safe it I did."

"But you want to go back."

I sighed. "At least to know that my other Ivan was safe."

"Your other Ivan?"

I shrugged. "What am I supposed to call him?"

"Ivan the turncoat?"

I bowed my head and smiled at the raw anger in his words. I knew it was directed at his other self for what had happened.

"It isn't fair to judge him. First, he was doing me a huge favor staying with me while that man was staked out."

"He stayed with you?"

I laughed softly, amused by his indignant tone. At least someone thought about the proprieties. "Yeah, in the guest room. But he disguised himself as my father, and I had hoped it would be enough to deter that man, but it wasn't."

"I don't look a thing like your father."

"No, and he was very creative."

"But he led them to you."

"Yes and no. He told Jackie, and he has had a crush on her since fifth grade. He didn't realize when he told her that it was her father who was hunting us."

Ivan sat up straighter. "Jackie who? I mean, theoretically she might be the same one that lives here."

"Jackie Sullen."

"Jacqueline Elliot Sullen?" he asked in measured tones.

"I suppose so. Yeah, her mother wanted to keep the Sullen line going, so she inverted Jackie's name or something, why do you know her?"

"Her and her father," he replied darkly.

"Oh, God, is her father the Mayor?"

"Yes."

"I'm so sorry."

"Don't be," he shook off his own demons and focused on mine. "Well, good to know bastards stay bastards. So, I stupidly have a crush on the serpent's daughter in your world? Wow, I must be an idiot."

I smiled a bit tentatively. "Yeah, I guess you could say that."

He puffed out his chest a little. "But you said I was your favorite."

"Always have been." I almost laughed at the smug expression on his face. "Does this mean you believe me?"

"I'll withhold judgment for now, but I'm willing to go on a little faith. No wonder you wanted me to spook your dad."

"Yeah, and it got more out of him than I think I've managed in the last three years." My lips pursed. "That was when he found Celeste. Eww."

"Would you look for your friends here?"

"What are you talking about? You're my only friend."

"I think Jimmy likes you now."

"Then I have two."

"You didn't answer my question."

"Didn't I? I told you I found you in other

worlds. There was never anyone else to look for. I only became popular my last few years when it became public knowledge that my house was adult free on weekends."

"And what did you do?"

I opened my mouth in incredulous shock, but noticed in time that he was laughing at me. "Not nice," I muttered.

"No one ever said I was nice," he replied with a cheeky grin.

"You were."

"That version of me also was an idiot, you said it yourself." He held up the mirror shard that he had kept with him. "Did you ask Jimmy to encase this?"

"He offered. I wanted to show it to my dad first, though."

"Is this how you'll find your grandmother?"

"I hope so."

"Well, I don't think you should be bleeding on it in public. I'll take it back to Jimmy on my way home. He should have it ready by your birthday. By the way, my mom wanted me to make sure you realized we wanted you to come. My brothers are only too happy that she's baking. They love her triple chocolate cake. You haven't suddenly developed an aversion to chocolate have you?"

"No," I said laughing at the image. "She really doesn't have to do anything."

"Don't tell her that. Anyway, I'll take you home tomorrow, if that's okay with you?"

"How do I get to school?"

He frowned, his fingers tapping along the iron bed frame as he thought. "Can you make it back to Merry Ave?"

"Yes."

"Good, if you go up two blocks to the Coffee Bean, there's a bus stop there. It leaves at seven twenty and it's usually pretty prompt."

"I think I can manage." I paused. "Will you be there?"

"Don't worry, Princess, I wouldn't want you to get lost on your first day." He went over to my window and looked out. "No offense, but I should really be leaving. It's dangerous even for a native to run down Current Street after hours. The police like to shoot first and ask questions second."

"You were alright yesterday."

"There were two of us, and you stand out as a safe beacon."

"Oh. Well, see you tomorrow then?"

"Yeah, see you then." He gave me a mock salute before shimmying down the trellis in record time. He picked up his jacket and bag before giving me another jaunty wave and heading off towards Shotgun Alley. Despite everything that had happened, I had to admit that it felt good to confide in someone and be believed, if only half heartedly.

SEVEN

Celeste had not moved when I got up for school the next day. I managed to boil water to make tea and toast was still pretty straight forward, so I was able to feed her and myself. I still wanted my Pop Tarts, but when it came right down to it, food was food. Still feeling out of my element, I also managed to figure out peanut butter and honey. I really needed to take Padma up on her offer to teach me to cook.

By the time I was done with feeding myself and Celeste, who seemed weakly grateful for the thought, though she wrinkled her nose at the toast, I was running really tight on time. Running around the neighborhood was getting to be a habit, and I bolted down the street for the coffee shop. The bus was pulling up as I huffed to a halt. There were a dozen other students waiting for it, only one looked my way. Ivan slipped an arm under mine to help me onto the bus.

"I thought you said this wouldn't be a problem for you," he said sarcastically.

I just glared, still too winded to manage any

words. The bus was full, but Ivan still found me a seat in the very back. There were more students and workers alike. As I caught my breath, I took in the diverse spectrum before me. It was obvious they were all from Shotgun Alley, but there was no one ethnicity. Instead, it seemed equally split along every ethnicity I could place. Some, like Ivan, were of mixed heritage, but whatever Shotgun Alley had been before the civil war, it certainly wasn't cookie cutter. Ivan must have been watching me closely because when I finally managed to breathe calmly, he started ribbing me again.

"You really need to stop running everywhere," he said. "People will get the wrong idea."

"What idea would that be?" I asked, rubbing my head. This wasn't good. It was seven thirty in the morning and I already had a headache.

"That we've left our borders," he replied, earning a wry smile from the woman sitting next to me. She agreed with him in a language I didn't understand, but he did, giving a rejoinder that had them both laughing.

"Oh, goody," I said darkly, "Now I'm the brunt of jokes I don't understand."

"Is that a new thing for you, Princess?"

I made a face at him and sat back with a huff. "You know what I just figured out? You're an ass."

"You just figured that out? And here I'd been trying so hard." He took pity on me, and patted my shoulder. "Sorry, I should give you at least a few days to learn that fact about me."

"Too late." I sighed. "Oh, wow, I just remembered today is my birthday." My mouth formed an "o" as I realized it was already Friday. What a crazy week. Just last Monday morning I had been worried only about whether or not my father and grandmother would show up for it. Seemed I wasn't going to get either.

"How does it feel?" asked Ivan, still watching me intently.

"No different. And let's be honest, my birthdays have sucked for the last five years."

"Well, I'm sure we'll make it better for you."

I made a face. "I have to start at a new school, my father has run away from home, and I am stuck with my future step mother who is currently comatose in her bed. Thanks, though, for the thought."

"You still going to be able to come over?"

"Yeah. I don't know what I was supposed to do, stay home with her? I'll call and check in, oh, no, scratch that. I don't know any numbers for her. Never mind, I'll try and do my best to forget my new found responsibilities."

He pursed his lips, but didn't say anything. We had come to another bus stop, and even more people crammed inside. He had to crowd my space, and I was squeezed into the personal space of the woman beside me. He apologized to her in her tongue, and she just smiled.

"Not new," she replied. "You should sit."

"I'm good," he replied.

"You will fall into her," she replied with a nod at me. Then she said something more I didn't understand, but it made him blush and he quickly squeezed in beside me. Rounding my shoulders in and making myself as small as possible, I tried to do my part. At least no one here was telling me I should lose weight to make more space. It didn't seem possible, but we made two more stops and no one was getting off. Finally, we stopped outside another bus station and Ivan pulled me off with him. He paid our fare and pulled me along to the back of the second bus. This one was much easier to find a seat on, and he sat down without protest. Everyone was dressed like us, girls in pleated gray skirts, white blouses, and pin striped jackets, boys in flat front slacks and blazers. Some had added splash, scarves seemed to be gender neutral, and, like Ivan, some complimented the outfit with a scarf and a hat. I felt out of place without a trace of personality added to mine. I took in the extras everyone had, trying to place what I would do without being too unoriginal. It seemed I'd have to get Celeste to take me shopping again.

This bus was the last of our interchange, and we only made one more pick up. Finally, after nearly an hour on the bus, it pulled up to a turn-in and we unloaded in mass. All three of the boys I had seen with skateboards gathered around Ivan, and two girls joined in. No one was quite willing to say anything, though, all watching me with curious suspicion.

We entered through cast iron gates and I stopped in my tracks. Everyone except Ivan kept walking as I took in the school I was to go to. My school had been cut and dry, cinder blocks, windows, a roof. This school had a face lift that made Celeste's kitchen look like a cheap Formica topped creation. Spires capped turrets on either side. Over the central entrance there was a magnificent stain glass to put Notre Dame's Cathedral to shame. The brick was a lovely shade of russet. The trees glistened around, quivering in the breeze. It looked like a castle, but the struggling ivy pointed to a recent remodel. The lawns were manicured, but I had a sneaking suspicion they were sod. It was all almost too beautiful to take in, and I had to blink several times to adjust my eyes to the brilliance.

"Ready?" asked Ivan the second I had adjusted.

"Yeah. As ready as I will be."

He smiled softly and led me inside. The interior did not match the exterior, though whoever was responsible for the planning had tried their best. Floors had carpeted runners, but the lockers were a glaring oddity, and the walls within were all new material. There was no lathing in these walls. Ivan pulled me along to the offices that sat to the right of the entrance. The windows were not antique either, but looked to be plastic or bullet proof glass. Slightly unsettled at the sight of metal detectors at the entrance to the offices, I hesitated and Ivan had to take my hand to lead me in. The main office had experienced a professional decorator's touch. There was no fiber board furniture, and the seats were all custom made and covered. Ivan lead me to the first desk, which was aged walnut where a regally coiffed silver haired woman sat. She put down the phone as we approached and her eyes quickly dismissed Ivan before falling to me.

"And who are you, my dear?"

"Nora Terre."

"Ah yes, Miss Winters called about you. If you'll wait a moment?" she pushed back and went to a filing cabinet at the back. Again, no detail had been missed in here. The cabinet was solid oak, if I had to guess, stained to match the rest of the dark wood furniture and complete with brass handles.

She wasn't long in getting my paper, clearly she had been expecting me. "Here is your class schedule," she said handing over one sheet, quickly followed by another. "And here is your locker and combination. If you would like a map, I can get one for you."

A little overwhelmed, I handed my schedule to Ivan. He looked over it and shook his head. "I can get you to your first four classes. Brad can get you to your last two."

"I don't need a map," I said politely, surprised at the expression the secretary was giving Ivan. "Thank you though."

She startled back to focusing on me. "Of course. Let me know if you need anything. I'll be happy to assign you another escort."

The venom dripped from her last words, and I took an involuntary step back, my shoulder bumping into Ivan. But my second thought was that she was insulting my friend. I took the step I had lost, and raised myself to my full height. "While I appreciate the offer, I am more content with the help I have."

If I hadn't been watching carefully I would have missed the faint lip curl. "Very well. Good luck, then."

I frowned but belatedly followed Ivan out. He took the slip that had my locker number and led the way to the left hall.

"'What was that about?" I asked as we weaved around students heading to class.

"She knows where I come from," he replied, stopping by the correct locker. Ironically, it was the same locker number I had in my other world. I opened it for kicks, not needing to look at the form to know the combination. I glanced at Ivan as I opened the blessedly empty space. He wasn't holding back the surprise.

"Same locker?" he asked carefully.

"Yeah, different school, same locker."

His eyebrows rose and fell, but he didn't say anything else, taking, instead, to watching other students move past us. Several nodded towards him, a few tried to stop to talk, but were pushed on by someone else. I watched this for a moment before remembering I had no purpose in opening my locker as I had no books for class. Shutting it, I turned to Ivan.

"So, where to?"

He handed me my schedule back. "First class is English, that's on the first floor, last room on the right."

"Do you have it too?"

"Yeah, and Chemistry after it. Your math class is right across the hall from my statistics class, so we'll be okay there. And then we have History. We'll get Brad to take you to Photography, that's in an out building, and after that it's back to the top floor for Spanish. He'll have those two with you." He lowered his lids, waiting for my answer. "Unless you want someone else."

"You're not the idiot one," I replied cheekily. "Come on, lead the blind."

He shook his head, but visibly relaxed and led the way to the last room. The woman behind the desk was tall, professional basketball player tall. Her black hair was kept short, and her eyes were like obsidian but her skin was paler than ivory. She looked up as we entered, and they widened slightly at the sight of me.

"And who might you be?" she asked, her voice a mixture of coldness masked by forced levity. She instantly made me nervous.

"Nora Terre."

"Ah, yes, Celeste's step daughter."

"Future step daughter," I corrected, but wished I'd swallowed the words when her black eyes flashed.

"Don't you like your future mother?"

"Of course," I replied, "but nothing's official yet."

"She's pregnant," replied the other woman. "Seems official to me."

I coughed in surprise, swallowing wrong and staying silent rather than try a response in my state of shock. Even with Ivan still beside me, I knew I'd be stuttering.

"Well, it is nice to meet you. Why don't you take a seat next to Amber?" she nodded to a pale red head. "I'll get you a book." She frowned at Ivan, and he took the silent message and went to his own seat. I tentatively took the seat that had been assigned. The rooms were less modern chic and more practical, but everything was still top of the line. The desks were in sets of two seats, and I was taking the only opening.

"Hi," I said a little awkwardly. Logic was screaming at me to watch my step. This was not the Amber I necessarily knew from before.

"Hi," she replied, her hazel eyes watching me closely as I took my seat. "Where are you from?"

"The other side of the world," I replied lightly.

"You don't sound Australian."

"My dad and I moved around a lot," I prevaricated.

"Oh, that sounds cool."

"Yeah, something like that."

She sat back, but the girl in front of us was trying to raise her eyebrows in silent communication, succeeding in only making her face look funny. I felt a little queasy to recognize another classmate, this one was Lara. Slender, blond, and blue eyed, she was a budding prima ballerina. Amber sighed, and looked back at me. "So, how do you know Ivan?"

"We were friends as kids," I replied, watching as the brunette a row up and over was conveyed this by Lara. Oh goody, Jacqueline Elliot Sullen was in my class. I glanced back at Ivan, but he was ignoring all of this, talking instead to the girl beside him. I felt a sudden stab of jealousy, but quashed that as quickly as it rose. Besides, I had more important things to focus on as Amber was continuing to ask me questions.

"What?"

"I said, where do you live?"

"Oh, up on Cherry Avenue. With my soon to be step mother."

"And who would that be?"

"Celeste Winters," I replied with a sigh. Why didn't the bell ring?

"Wow, well, welcome to Golden Gate Academy."

"Thanks,"

"What's your next class?"

"Chemistry."

"Oh," her face fell, and she kicked the back of Lara's seat. "I have Geometry next. Lara too. Stephen has Chemistry though, doesn't he?"

Lara turned and nodded. "So does Tyler.

Would you like us to get them to take you?"

"Uh, no, I'm good, thanks."

"I'm Lara, by the way."

"Hi," I said, curbing the instant response of "I know." "I'm Nora."

She smiled brilliantly, and I felt a tiny sigh escape Amber. It seems some things didn't change. "Nice to meet you. What's after that for you?"

I recited my class schedule, and found that I had three with the "in" crowd. Both girls offered me an escort to my others, but I reiterated I was okay when finally the bell rang.

My Chemistry teacher was the same person, and I had to bite my tongue as I was assigned Brad as my lab partner. Everything about Mr. Dawson was the same, his flyaway gray hair, his sparkling blue eyes, and his exuberant teaching style. Ivan and the girl he had been seated with in English were at the station next to us as we were given silver nitrates to observe.

"So, Nora," said Brad with a wicked grin towards Ivan who was pretending not to notice. "It's so nice to finally meet you. Lucky for you Jackie pulled out of Chemistry after Maria set her braid on fire."

The other girl, who I recognized from the coffee shop and the train ride cried out in protest. "For the hundredth time, I didn't mean to, and who flips their hair while their playing with a Bunsen burner?"

Brad just chuckled and pointed his pencil at Ivan. "Depends on who they're flirting with."

Ivan rolled his eyes and continued to write rather than acknowledge them. I made notations about the reaction going on in front of me, feeling an odd sense of deja-vu. Mr. Dawson was not only the same person, his lesson plan was the same. He came up half way through class and handed me a detailed syllabus.

"Nora, I thought you might like to know what we've been covering, just in case your other teacher hadn't covered any of this."

I glanced at the paper, going pale, but smiling all the same. "No, this looks pretty similar."

"Smart teacher you have then," he replied with a grin, leaving us to our work.

"You have no idea," I muttered, surprised to hear Ivan chuckle. Looking over at me, he glanced pointedly to Mr. Dawson and back to me. I nodded, and he covered his second laugh with a cough, as we had attracted the attention of the others. By the time that hour was over, I was friends with two more people, but even Brad backed down when it came to who was taking me to Calculus.

"What about Mrs. Ives?" Ivan asked as he guided me up the stairs.

"No, she's different. My English teacher was a sarcastic, balding man who actually liked me. She's harsh, and I don't think I made points."

He shook his head, stopping at the top of the stairs to let two girls go past. Both were sighing over him. I had to stifle the laugh at his obliviousness. "Most of the teachers are connected to the Board, which runs off the puppet strings of the Mayor's office. I think your future step mom is connected, but I can't place how. I've tried to forget all that crap."

"Understandable," I replied.

"How many students are the same?" he asked,

opening the door for me.

"So far? At least fifteen. I've never met Maria or Brad, but the others, yeah, they're the same."

"Well, good luck here, Mrs. Ridley can be a bit of a tough nut, but you should be fine."

"Oh, right, your class is Statistics. Lucky you."

He shrugged. "It looks good on an application and I finished Calc last year. Let me know, by the way, if you need any help." He stepped back as other students filed in. I went with the flow, only to come face to face with yet another teacher I recognized. Mrs. Ridley was short, slim, and not to be messed with. Her blue eyes were hidden behind thick glasses, and her dark blond hair was kept severely back.

"You must be Nora," she said as I came to a stop in front of her. "Word travels fast when we get a new student." She paused, and I had the sneaking suspicion she was leaving something unsaid. "Well, let me get you a book, and let's get you seated. Don't worry for the next few days, I won't expect you to do the homework. Just get a feel, and by next Wednesday, we'll see where you are."

Despite the complexity of the material, this was my easiest class by far. I recognized a few people, but no one I was going to introduce myself to. I had been shy at school, and I was content to keep it that way. However, one of the boys caught up with me as the bell rang.

"Hey, I'm Stephen," he said, falling in step beside me. "Where are you headed?"

I knew Stephen, he was one of the top jocks, leading receiver for the football team and all around really cool guy. He had never spared ten words for me before. We were dangerously close to beating that.

"History."

"I'll take you, I have the same."

I looked over my shoulder uneasily to see Ivan coming out of his class. Stephen caught the direction of my gaze and pulled me along rather than allowing me to linger.

"I promise not to get you lost. Besides, Lara asked me to check in on you. And since you're new, we'll want to take care of you, at least until you get your bearings."

"Okay," I said slowly, not able to really put up a fight. He was at least six three, and his hands were like iron. "I was really okay before."

He stopped and opened the door for me. "Maybe, maybe not. Come on, Mr. Engel won't mind where you sit."

Feeling like a rag doll, I managed to win out on obstinacy alone. I stopped by the front desk, sans teacher, and defiantly waited. Stephen must have noticed the mulish expression on my face, for he let me go and went to sit with Amber and Jackie.

Slowly, the rest of the class filtered in, and I was surprised that I was standing directly in the middle of an invisible line. One half of the class were my bus mates, the others all revolved around Jackie. I was surprised to find Brad on the popular side. He was sitting with Ivan as an informal bridge, but there were no seats in the invisible line other than Brad's. It was like a mine field that no one would cross. So far, my other classes had had seat assignments with no submission to these unspoken rules, but when left to their own devices, even though we were all dressed alike, everyone instinctively went back to their own. Mr. Engel came in with the bell, and his round face lit up at the sight of me.

"Ah, you must be Nora Terre." He shook my rather limp fingers. "So nice to meet you my dear. Why don't you take a seat? Here's a book, we're just about to the Continental Congress. Are you familiar with that?"

I nodded mutely. Freaky, but this was the second class in one day that I was exactly on time for the source material. Mrs. Ridley had been a few days ahead of where I was, but only Mrs. Ives had differed drastically. This version of Mr. Engel was slimmer, but everything else, right up to the three hairs worth of comb over were the same.

"Excellent, well, here you go, take your pick," he said, gesturing to the room.

I could feel my face turning red, and a faint line of sweat appeared on my brow line. However, rather than make any sort of statement, I was forced by necessity to take a seat in the no man's land. I sat in front of Brad and Ivan, next to Lara on one side and Maria on the other. They both smiled, but when they caught their equally warm greetings, they both turned away from me. Sighing, I opened my book to the right chapter without looking at the index and waited for class to begin. At least then there was some peace.

Lunch was equally difficult. I had my crude PB&J but I was being fought over for who got to sit with me. I tried to find Ivan, but he wasn't in the cafeteria, and while Maria made a move for me, it was none other than Jackie that won. With a face that looked like an innocent child, and the attitude of a fox, she was bound to win at most things she tried.

"Nora, everyone else has had a chance to meet you, but I haven't. Please, come and join me."

I sighed and let myself be pulled away by her. Sitting down between Amber and Jackie, I waited to eat until she had started her subtle interrogation.

"How have classes been so far?" she asked.

"Good, I guess," I replied, wondering why she started so banally.

"You know, Amber says you have Photography next. You can come with me." She tossed her silky black hair and looked at the others with a faint air of challenge. "They all decided to learn to cook instead."

"That's never been my strong suit," I replied wryly.

"Mine either," she replied with equal levity. I couldn't quite place the Jackie I knew with this version. A part of her spoke to me of similar experiences. It was almost as if she were a kindred spirit, and it felt odd to think that one should be and the other would be my antithesis. "Do you like photography or is it just an elective for you?"

"I love it," I replied earnestly.

"Wonderful! I have a Canon 30mm, its old and my parents buy me new ones every year, but it gets the best picture."

I could have been bowled over with a finger. "Celeste bought me an Olympus for my birthday yesterday."

"Oh, was yesterday your birthday?"'

"No, today is."

"Well, we should do something for you!"

"I have plans for today," I said, surprised at my own apology.

Jackie's lips pursed, but she smiled at the

others. "How about Saturday? I know we just met, so I shouldn't overwhelm you. Do you like French pastries?"

"Never tried one," I replied.

"But I thought you traveled with your dad."

"I did, just not to France. I'm sure I would. My food has been pretty limited to what comes out of a box."

She smiled slowly, and as she had finished, she pulled me from our audience. "I've always wanted to try those frozen pizza bites. Our cook won't let them in the house, but there's just something so normal, you know?"

"Yeah, they're not bad, but I'd suggest the frozen taquitos. Those are my favorite."

She was leading me outside, and slowly filing out behind us were the others. She sighed as she watched them. "Sometimes I just want to get away from this all," she said wistfully. "Eat junk food, stay in my pjs all day."'

She was describing my life to a "t". "I don't know how Celeste would handle that," I said carefully, "but that's how I lived for the last five years. We could try it sometime."

"That would be wonderful," she said, it astounded me to see the honesty shining through her eyes, but in another second it was gone, replaced by the cunning I knew so well. "So, how well do you know Ivan Battuta?"

"Ivan? We've been friends since we were kids."

"Oh, and that's all?"

"Yeah. I visited until I was twelve."

A shadow flitted across her face. In a second it was gone, replaced by the sunny smile. "That was a rough year for a lot of us."

I nodded, waiting for the next zinger.

"What are your plans for your birthday? I'm sure Celeste wouldn't mind if a few of us joined you."

"Oh, my plans aren't with Celeste. Or, far as I can tell, my father."

Her dark eyes narrowed, but her sunny expression never changed. "Then who? And where?"

"I don't know, somewhere in Shotgun Alley. Ivan's mom is baking me a cake."

"Really? Are you certain I can't come with you?"

"Well, I would hate to impose on her, and I really don't know what's going on anyway. She volunteered, and I accepted. It's all a little last minute. I'm sure you could come to my house tomorrow. Celeste shouldn't mind."

"Of course not," she said, but there was a faint hint of disappointment. "Well, we should have a sleep over, then. I'll bring the pastries. What about the others?"

"Amber, Lara, and Krystal?" I asked.

"Have you met Krystal?"

I hadn't, at least not here, but I knew she was one of them. "Maybe she was pointed out by Stephen," I said carefully.

"That would make sense. All of her ex-boyfriends like to point her out."

"That must be a lot of boys," I said before catching myself. "I'm sorry, I didn't mean that."

But she was laughing and watching as Krystal tossed her perfectly coifed hair in Brad's direction. "No, but it's true. You certainly catch on fast. Anyway, that sounds like fun." She looked over my shoulder and her lips twitched towards a frown. "Unless you think I might get an invite tonight."

Glancing over my shoulder, I saw Ivan and a few of his friends coming up to the school. "I don't think so."

"You're right," she said, taking my arm and steering me back inside. "Ivan has never been the party boy, and certainly not with me. Well, come on, we should start off towards class. It'll be so wonderful to have someone who cares about photography."

I let her lead me on, disappointed not to be able to talk to Ivan, but when Jackie had made up her mind, she was hard to distract. Miss Reynolds was new to me, and I appreciated the change. My old teacher had been too concerned with her own art to bother actually teaching us anything useful. Jackie and I joined up with Brad and Krystal for Spanish. It was pointless for me, as I had finished three years and here I was back in second year. However, it meant I had one cakewalk of a class to look forward to. It was nice to know that somewhere in my life, I could just take a breather. I was going to need it.

EIGHT

When class was finally over, I wasn't surprised to find that my locker was already a mess. I opened it to pull out my History and English, but everything else fell on me instead. Reaching down to pick up the mess, someone joined me.

"I see you made friends," said Ivan in measured tones.

"They found me," I replied, scooping up everything I could and throwing it back in. Ivan came behind and carefully placed the rest in.

"You should really try and keep this organized. I think you've set a new record here."

"Like I haven't heard that before," I muttered. "Here, make yourself useful and put your hand here." I placed his hand on the top of the pile and pulled out the bottom book. He pulled his hand slowly away and I slammed the locker shut.

"Did I tell you that before?" he asked as we made our way back to the buses.

"As a matter of fact, yes. And you also are the only one I know who can get anything out without it all falling over. Give me a few days and I'll establish my system of chaos."

"I think you already have."

"Haha." We loaded up and took our seats at the back. At the interchange, I had a few people I now knew to say good bye to. He just gave a general wave and pulled me along to our crowded bus. He managed to squeeze me into a seat at the middle, politely thanking the diminutive old man who had moved over.

"How many languages do you speak?" I asked as we rattled along. Again, I hadn't understood a word, and, again, they had laughed in my direction.

"Four. The Village is a bit of a melting pot. It's easiest to know what's being said, saves on problems later."

The old man nodded in agreement.

"Which four?" I asked.

"Spanish, Hindi, English, and some Ukrainian. I've picked up on some Chinese and Vietnamese as well as some useful Russian."

"Wow," I said, and I meant it.

"He's useful to have around, your boyfriend," said the woman on the other side of me.

"Oh," I was stalled out of speech by my own nervousness. Ivan watched and waited for me to say something, but I couldn't form the words. Every time I tried, I could feel them tripping on my tongue.

"Catch that Princess," he said as we were jostled by another stop. "I'm useful." The woman had exited and he took her seat when no one else loaded on.

"You didn't correct her," I said, blushing.

"I thought you would."

"I can't. Not always."

He nodded, leaning back and taking a cursory scan of the bus. "You still stutter?"

"Sometimes. When I get upset or flustered."

"You did a pretty good job laying into me the last few days."

"You're different."

"Ah, careful, that'll go to my head."

"It already has," I groused.

"Probably." But he was inordinately smug for the rest of the ride.

We got off on the opposite side of the street as the Coffee Bean. He pulled me across the street and took me inside. We were greeted by no less than five strangers and two people I knew by sight, but not by name.

"Quite the hang out," I said dryly. He ignored me and went to the counter. The waitress that had flirted with Jimmy the day before smiled a little too brightly. I rolled my eyes and turned away so I wouldn't have to watch. Standing at the window, I watched people come and go, noticing that there were several fellow students, but mostly they were working people. Those who were dressed nicely were always given a second glance. Ivan came back and handed over a Styrofoam cup.

"You ready?"

"I guess."

He held the door open and let me out. I took a sip of my drink, surprised to find that it was exactly what I had ordered with Jimmy. Suspiciously, I glanced over at him. He was ignoring me in favor of his own drink. "Happy birthday, by the way, Princess."

"Thanks. And thanks for the drink."

He shrugged, looking both ways before starting across the street. "Come on, keep up."

We made fast time to the Merry Ave intersection, and he stopped me when I would have walked on. Holding out a package, I unfolded the paper bag to find a cell phone in it.

"What is this?"

"Don't you have cell phones in your world?"

"Of course we do," I replied with an exaggerated eye roll. "But why give me one?"

"I asked for a favor from a friend," he replied. "It's a burner, the best we can manage to get around here. Reception ends where the electricity does, so, here," he handed me a piece of paper, "call your house, leave a message, ditch the phone."

"Aren't you just full of surprises?" I asked in awe. He had provided me with two numbers, and I called the first, getting the answering machine and Celeste's voice. I frowned, feeling like I should really talk to a human. Calling the second, I resigned myself to leaving a message when she picked up.

"Hello?"

"Celeste?"

"Who is this?"

"It's Nora."

"Oh, Nora, how was school?" she was clearly exhausted. I was impressed she managed to remember who I was let alone that I had gone to school.

"Fine, look, I've been invited over for an early dinner, but I wanted to make sure you were okay."

"Thank you, dear. Have a good time."

She hung up on me. This surprised me ever so

slightly. Handing the phone over to Ivan, I smiled gamely.

"Well, that worked out."

"Your dad's still not home?"

"Guess not."

He frowned and savagely pulled the phone apart, depositing half of it in the garbage and crushing the other half under his boots. Despite our strict uniform code, he kept his boots, and when no one was watching, he kept the slacks tucked into them. I had noticed that partway through the day, his hat had been removed, but it was back now, and the whole statement was almost comical if not for the fact that half of the students made similar statements. I had a feeling it would be dangerous to laugh at them all.

Ivan led me down a different street than he had the night before, and branched off the beaten path up half a block to an oddly placed house. It was set away from the main blocks of bullet ridden town houses, but it certainly had not been spared. The tree out front, a true rarity, was dead, cracked down the center with brilliant black marks down its center split. The lower story windows were barred. The upper stories were boarded up. Here, rather than the sparkling brilliance of the blue skies, it all seemed enveloped in its own gloom. A few clouds were gathering overhead, and the whole thing reminded me of something from one of Edgar Allen Poe's stories.

At my hesitation, Ivan took hold of me and pulled me up the stairs. The front door was opened by two miniature versions of him. They jumped out and climbed up him like monkeys. Crying out in a language that was neither English nor Spanish, they hugged him as though they hadn't seen him in ages. He gently extracted himself, correcting them in their other tongue.

"Len, Ajay, manners." They let go with a sigh, and stood at attention, watching their brother in anticipation. "This is Nora; Nora, these are my brothers, Len," he nodded to the shorter one, "and Ajay."

I smiled and held out my hand. Ajay took it with great gravity. He gave a little bow over my hand.

"A pleasure to meet you, Nora."

"And you, as well, Ajay," I replied, trying not to laugh.

"Len and Ajay are enrolled at the Rosaria Academy. It has a strong emphasis on the arts, particularly acting."

"How old are they?" I asked despite myself.

"Len is seven, Ajay is ten."

"We're standing right here," said Ajay with a frustrated whine.

"Yeah, I know that. Go tell Mom we're here."

Ajay hesitated, ready to argue, but Ivan pushed him on up the stairs.

"They're cute. I always wanted a sibling." I couldn't stop smiling as we watched them scamper off.

"Really? Why?" He sighed and started up the old stairs.

I shrugged and followed up him. "I had a very lonely childhood."

"Siblings hardly solve that when they're so much younger than you are. They occupy your time in ways I'd rather not discuss."

"Well, any chance you could break it to me

sooner rather than later? Last time I checked, I have three months to get ready for it."

He stopped half way up, turning back to laugh at me. "I guess you're right. I didn't think about it like that. Well, there's the sleepless nights, the dirty diapers, teething, feeding, burping, washing, and getting them to sleep. None of it is fun. You should hope Celeste does most of it. My mom did, but we're all on one floor, and the walls here aren't that great. And then my mom came down with a staph infection. That's when it fell to me. At least with Len. I didn't have much to do with Ajay except getting him to eat, sleep, and changing his diapers. I would happily not have had that personal experience. Lucky you."

"Yeah, lucky me. Still, you love them right?"

"Of course. They're family." We had reached the landing for the middle level. He opened the main door and held it for me. "By the way, if Celeste is your mother, does that mean she's carrying you?"

"No, thank God. Kid's a boy."

"Oh, that would have been awkward. And disturbing."

"Tell me about it."

"Ivan?" Padma peered around the corner, wiping her hands on her apron. "Nora! So good to see you, come in, you're a little early, or I'm a little late, but, please make yourself at home."

"Thank you."

She waved away my thanks and went back into the kitchen. The boys came and sat on either side of me in the cramped living room. A couch, a love seat, and an arm chair had somehow managed to fit in the ten by twelve space. Len, Ajay, and I were now squeezed into the sofa.

"Ivan says you come from far away," said Ajay. "Like Africa?"

"Or China?" asked Len.

"No, I'm not really from that far away. I've just been to a lot of places."

"Like Africa?"

"No, I've never been to Africa."

"Oh," both boys looked crestfallen. "Anywhere exciting?"

If Ajay had been a little younger, I might have told them about the Second Realm where dinosaurs still roamed, but I didn't think ten was young enough to not ask awkward questions. "Well, I went to a place where they live like knights in castles."

"Really? Did they fight?"

"All the time."

"And real armor?"

"As far as I could tell."

"Cool."

"Anywhere cooler?"

"Um, I once went to a wildlife preserve. Lots of animals."

"Like lions?"'

"Yeah, and tigers and bears. Even elephants and giraffes."

"Then you have been to Africa."

"Something like Africa."

Someone knocked at the door, and Ivan, who had been laughing at my expense for the questioning, went to answer. Jimmy and Sofia came in with the young boy who had been supervising the kids. I waved from my spot, but Len landed on my leg before I could even think of getting up.

"Tell me more about Africa."

Jimmy came in and sat on the single chair. Len, apparently, was easily distracted. He bounded over to Jimmy and pounced him instead.

"Hey, Nora," said Jimmy as he fended off Len. "How was your first day at school?"

"Better than I expected."

"It'll get worse."

"Such optimism."

"I like to see it as realism," he replied. Jorge, the boy who had been supervising at the pot luck, came in and corralled the two Battuta boys with a look of the deepest resignation. "Did Mom assign you?" asked Jimmy.

"Yeah. I thought I was coming over to eat cake."

"You will, but this one," he said with a playful noogie to Len, "needs supervision."

"I don't," protested Ajay.

"Hey, your mom sent me."

"Well, I'll have to discuss that particular issue with her," Ajay said with such pomp I had to smile.

When they were gone, Jimmy moved to sit beside me. "I don't have much time to tell you this, so I'll be as quick as I can. I found where that mark comes from. It's an abandoned factory on Finch Island."

"Really? Can I get there?"

He frowned mightily at me. "I don't think that's a good idea."

"Why not?"

"There is nothing left on Finch Island. It was where most of the Third Ward worked before the assassination. It was destroyed after. There's still a few places that are open for business, but its not a safe place to go."

"But I need to go there. I have to find whatever I can."

"Well," he sighed and ran a hand through his hair, bowing his head and trying to consider all his options. "The ferry only runs out there on weekdays. There's one over in the morning and one back at night."

"What time?"

"Nora, I can't tell you that. Ivan would have my head if I let you go."

"Jimmy, I'm going. You could always come with me."

But he just shook his head. "I'll head over on Monday, I have the night shift, I should be able to make it back on time. I'll see what I can find, but that's it."

I frowned, and collapsed back into the sofa. Behind me, I heard a few more people coming in. Turning, I saw Brad and Maria along with the other two skate boarders, Mike and Luca. Ivan brought them into the room where we were and took the arm rest on my other side.

"What's going on?" he asked smoothly.

"Nothing," replied Jimmy, but he didn't meet Ivan's eyes when he said it.

"What do you know about Finch Island?" I asked the others. Maria jumped to go help catch Len who was running around the apartment without a shirt on. Brad took one look at Ivan and ran after her.

"Why do you want to know?" asked Ivan.

Jimmy was trying to edge off the sofa, but Ivan stopped him with a look.

"I need to see if anyone knows about the maker of my mirror."

The added meaning this explanation held for Ivan registered openly on his face and he settled deeper into the sofa, sliding off the arm rest. "Oh, well, the ferries only run Monday thru Friday."

Jimmy's draw dropped. "You're going to let her go there?"

Ivan raised one smooth brow incredulously. "Do you honestly think I could stop her? There might be a midnight shift ferry back. If there is, we could go after school Monday, be back by midnight, hopefully."

I smiled radiantly and hugged him. His surprise was evident, but he awkwardly patted my shoulder all the same. "You're the best," I said, sitting back.

"I am, aren't I?"

"I can't make that time," said Jimmy. "I've got the night shift up at the packaging plant."

"We'll be fine, but at least if we don't come home, you'll know where to look."

"Right," he said uneasily. "You do know what you're doing, don't you?"

"Of course."

We were saved from anything more by Padma announcing the cake was finished. It was only four thirty in the afternoon, but I was only too happy to eat to my heart's content. I was amazed to find myself enjoying my little party. I was naturally so shy, I had avoided parties my entire life, but Ivan's mother hardly changed. She always made sure that I had something to look forward to.

It was growing dark by the time everyone had left. Padma kept glancing absently out the window, a worried frown creasing her face in well worn lines.

"Ivan, I think you should be leaving." She took to nibbling on her nail in agitation. "It's Friday, you know how they get about the streets on Fridays."

He nodded, getting to his feet and waiting for me to do the same. "Come along, Princess. I don't want to be jumped coming home."

The two younger boys were off playing cowboys and aliens or something similar. Their happy cries contrasted sharply with the atmosphere in the dining room.

"Isn't there a way I could help?"

Both shook their heads in unison.

"It is what it is, Nora. We've learned to adapt," said Padma sadly. "Go on, you should be safe with Ivan."

I gathered my bag, but on an impulse, I turned back around and hugged her. 'Thank you, for everything. This was wonderful. You always make things right."

She returned the embrace gently. "It was no trouble, my dear. My offer still stands for cooking lessons, if you're free on Sundays."

"I think I'll be free as a bird unless something drastic changes," I said wryly. "Can I be trusted to find my way back?" I challenged Ivan. He, however, gave the question serious consideration.

"I'll come get you on Sunday. Maybe after that the village will accept you, word spreads quickly, but better safe than sorry."

"I'll take that. Everything was wonderful, Mrs. Battuta."'

"Please, call me Padma. I'll see you on Sunday,

then, and happy birthday, dear."

I waved to the boys, but they barely noticed. Ivan kept me close as we made our way out of the closed in streets. When Merry Ave was in view, he let go of me and walked alongside, hands in his pockets. He, at least, had been able to change out of his uniform.

"Jimmy was right to be worried about Finch Island," he said, holding me back from crossing as a Vespa breezed by. "Only the stubbornest survived out there after the crackdown. And they don't take kindly to outsiders."

"Don't they know you?"

"Even if they do, some of them won't take to me. I might actually be more of a hindrance than a help."

"Why?"

He frowned, kicking a crack of concrete along. "Has someone told you my family's disgrace?" he asked caustically.

"If you mean has anyone told me about what happened to make Shotgun Alley what it is, yes, Jimmy told me yesterday."

He raised his eyes to the darkening sky. "Figures. Anyway, most of the Village took me and my family in, no questions asked, treated us like we were one of their own, but a few saw it differently. When Finch Island was included in the casualty list, most of the workers blamed the Village for it. They were innocent, its just that once the Mayor got it in his head to punish us, he didn't stop at anything."

I put out my hand and pulled him to a stop. "You were all innocent bystanders," I said softly.

"Someone was guilty."

"You don't think it was your father?"

"No," he shook his head sharply. "My dad had issues with the Deputy Mayor, Jackie's father, not the Mayor. And whoever fired that shot, there was no doubt who they were aiming for."

"You won't let me go alone, will you?"

"Hardly. They might hate me, but they'll definitely hate you."

"That's comforting."

"Jimmy could always go on his own and tell us what he finds. He's the safest option."

"No, if there is something out there, I would have to explain this all to him."

"Don't you like Jimmy?"

"Of course I do, but you have to admit, it would be pretty hard to swallow."

"It is hard to swallow, Princess, and I trust you. Alright, I'll double check the ferry times. We'll probably have to go straight there from school. It'll take at least another two bus interchanges to get there, and then the ferry. There's only one out and one back. If we miss it, we have to try again."

"Then we'll have to make sure we don't miss it."

"That's the spirit." He stopped and looked up at my house. "No trellis climbing?"

"Not in a skirt!"

"Oh, right," he shrugged and grinned at me. "I promise I wouldn't look."

"Thanks, for that resounding guarantee, but I'll take the front door. Do you want to come in?"

"No, I should be heading back. Lights go off half an hour earlier on Fridays and Saturdays. And the police will be out in force. Best I hurried."

"Then thank you," I said. "And I'll see you

Sunday?"

"Yeah, is one good for you?"

"Should be."

"I'll try the back entrance, then."

"That's a good idea. I'll leave my window cracked. Let yourself in if I'm not there."

He shook his head and turned to go home, walking backwards to still face me. "You have to admit, this conversation sounds a little crazy."

"Just a little?"

"Right, happy birthday, Nora."

"Thank you, Ivan."

He nodded, his crooked smile still playing around his mouth, before pivoting and taking off at a jog back towards Merry Ave. I let myself in, surprised to find my camera on the kitchen counter with a small serving of still warm lasagna. Celeste came in from the living room to see who it was. She smiled somewhat tentatively.

"Thank you for tea this morning," she said. She took the bowl and moved to the microwave to reheat it. "I wasn't sure what you wanted, and I figured your friends made you cake. You do like lasagna, don't you?"

It hurt to realize that this proverbial stranger who so represented someone I had loved had remembered my birthday and my own father hadn't.

"I love it." I got myself a water bottle and took a seat as she placed the reheated food at the kitchen bar. "Are you going to join me?"

Her hands fluttered uncertainly, but even though she was emotionally spent, there was the first trace of something like camaraderie between us.

"If you don't mind."

"Not at all."

It was a quiet but not unpleasant meal. The longer I talked to her, the more I remembered little traits of my mother. She, too, had been prone to an emotional roller coaster. My father had absorbed most of her ups and downs, as he had absorbed most of her. She was no more my mother than this Ivan was my other Ivan, but they shared so much, it was easy to fall into a pattern of open affection. Celeste was a little rougher to handle when she was telling me I was fat, but I figured it wouldn't hurt me to try. After all, I was stuck here for the foreseeable future, and maybe, just maybe, this was where I wanted to be.

NINE

On the whole, it was a pretty good birthday. No one had died, more than one person had remembered. It was a low bar, but the lower the bar, the easier it was for the world to succeed by my low standards of it.

The next day, I remembered in time that I had even more company arriving. It was a new and slightly terrifying prospect. Celeste had been thrilled to hear I was having friends over, especially when she learned who they were. She went above and beyond for the food preparations, and by the time Jackie arrived, the house was spotless to boot.

I was struck dumb at the arrival of the four girls. There was no easy way for me to be around them, afraid of what I might say or who I was supposed to be, but they didn't seem to need me to make themselves comfortable. They had brought their own sleeping bags, and after everyone changed into their pjs, we gathered around and watched horror movies. I hated horror movies, they kept me awake with nightmares for at least four days after watching just one, but I couldn't unhinge my mouth to say those words. As the evening wore on, though, I found myself growing more comfortable, and by the time Amber, Lara, and Krystal had fallen asleep, I was more than ready to have a good, solid conversation.

"Not much of a 'fright night' sort of person are you?" asked Jackie, who was the only one besides myself still awake.

I looked down at my hands which still had a death grip on my sleeping bag that Celeste had provided. Slowly, I unclenched each resisting finger. "What gave you that idea?" I asked.

She laughed softly and pulled her knees to her chest. "I wasn't at first either, but Amber, I swear, won't watch anything else. What's your favorite movie?"

Feeling a little foolish, I stared at my toes when I answered. *"Beauty and the Beast."*

"The Disney version?"

"Yeah. I've watched a few others, like the French one that everyone raves about, but it's singing candlesticks for me."

"Don't tell them," she said with a gesture to the snoring forms around us, "but my favorite is the *Little Mermaid.* I see your singing candlestick and raise you a singing crab."

I had to stuff my fist in my mouth to catch the laugh that bubbled out. I wondered if this was the real Jackie, if I had never gotten to know her before, or if she was truly this different. "I have most of the Disney movies," I said, but paused. I had *had* them. "I'm not sure they've arrived yet," I said quickly. "If they're anywhere, they'd be upstairs in the guest room."

She followed me up as we crept first around the

others and then slowly up the stairs. We were both repressing giggles, and I pulled her into my room for a quick laugh break. She understood without asking, and when we had gotten it out of our system, we crept along the hall. I cautiously opened the door, not a hundred percent positive what I would find. Of all the rooms in the house, this one hadn't had an ounce of remodeling. It was exactly like my guest room, which meant it housed a futon, a wardrobe and a television. I was surprised Celeste hadn't ventured in here with her designer's touch, but when I opened the wardrobe and found all of my movies, I didn't really care.

"Wow, you have *The Great Mouse Detective*. I thought I was the only person who had that."

I smiled, and let her choose. "My dad still buys me Disney movies for my birthday. I tried once to tell him I wanted something else, but he ignored me and bought every movie released that year."

She sighed and pulled *Snow White* out. "I know the feeling. My dad never listens to a word I say. Neither does my mother. I can't wait until I'm eighteen and can go live with my sister." That answered my question. This Jackie was definitely different.

"I always wanted to take a car across the country, take pictures, shoot some film, turn it into a short film. Maybe win Cannes."

She laughed and handed over *Cinderella*. "I think we should try for Sundance. When we're eighteen, we should definitely do that."

I had never made such a promise in my life, I was never so confident as to where I would be or what I would be saddled with in a year. But in that moment, I felt some part of my heart flutter free.

"When's your birthday?"

"April."

"Then we should aim for after graduation. We have the cameras, we just need a car."

"And a map."

"Yeah, and a map."

She sat down as I started the movie, and I could tell she wasn't really with me. "What is it like?" she asked quietly as the movie started.

""What is what like?"

"Well, being able to travel?"

"In my experience, it's not all it's cracked up to be, but it's been years since I went anywhere I wanted to."

"Didn't you want to come here?"

"At first, no, but I did miss some of it."

She glanced slyly at me out of the corner of her eye. "Like Ivan?"

"Like Ivan."

"So, tell me, what is it between the two of you? Are you dating?"

I held in a nervous chuckle. "No."

"Do you want to?"

"Right now, I just want to fit in."

She sighed, and propped her feet up on the foot stool in front of us. "Fitting in isn't all its cracked up to be."

I smiled at the similarities and mimicked her posture. We watched the movie in silence, and I felt more comfortable than I had been all day. By the time it was two in the morning, we were onto *Sleeping Beauty,* and Jackie had fallen asleep. I was much more relaxed than I had been, but was still too jumpy to sleep after three straight horror movies. Two Disney movies were not enough to counter horror. Prince Philip was about to slay the dragon Maleficent when I heard the door open down stairs. Jumping straight out of my seat, I felt all the fear so recently banished return in full force. Cautiously, I crept to the door, tiptoeing down the hall. I was trying to see something in pitch black, and it wasn't working. Someone swore below me and turned on a light.

"Dad?"

He looked up the stairs and swore. "Nora, what are you doing here?"

"I live here, remember?"

He seemed so lost. I hurried down, years of training over powering my ever growing frustration. "Come on, I have company."

"You have what?"

"Company. Friends."

"But you just got here."

"Thanks, Dad." I had nowhere else to go but my bedroom or the bathroom. Bedroom won that. "Where have you been?"

"I told you I had to go see about your grandmother," he said, but something was off in his words. I hadn't lived with my father for seventeen years not to know when something was off. And he looked like he had been mugged in seven different countries.

"Any luck?"

"No, but maybe in a few more days."

He was hedging, but I couldn't tell why. "Maybe you should be getting to bed. You look awful."

He glanced over at me, a rare smile tugging the corners of his mouth. "Thanks, Nora."

I shrugged. "Are you staying this time?"

"For awhile at least. I know this wasn't what was supposed to happen, but I hope we can work on our relationship. I want you to like Celeste."'

"That's not the problem," I said, crossing my arms across my chest. "Do you realize what Friday was?"

"Was? Did I miss your birthday?"

"Right in one."

"I'm so sorry, Nora, but I had some things to take care of."

I wanted to cry, and hit something, not necessarily in that order. Instead, I wrenched my door open and stared pointedly at the hall. "There always is. Good night, Dad."

He hesitated in the doorway, but when he didn't immediately say something, I shut the door on him. I had thought for years that my mother's death had rattled him too badly to be a good father to me. I was right, but I had imagined him holed up in his own grief, not out knocking up another version of her.

I sat on my bed with a huff, trying to think what I would do if I was in his position. It occurred to me that I had traveled through Portals and found different versions of Ivan, did that count as the same thing? Just because I hadn't abandoned my family to do it, didn't mean the possibility wasn't still there. Filled with the deepest sense of self loathing, I went back to catch the end of *Sleeping Beauty*. I adjusted Jackie on the couch so she was more comfortable and put the throw over her. I hadn't been picking up after my father wherever he crashed not to know how to do this without waking her. I went to my own bed to sleep, but I had a hard time of it. The sky was startling to sparkle with aquamarine streaks by the time my exhaustion over took me.

Jackie's mother arrived at eight in the morning. I was startled awake by the door bell. Blinking through the stupor, I stumbled down the stair and opened the door with only one eye open.

"Can I help you?" I asked miserably. My wavy blond hair was sticking up at the top, my patch on the crown of my head that marched to the beat of its own drum was standing as straight up as twenty four inches of hair could, and it hurt to have both eyes open. On top of all that, I was in flannel, polar bear themed pajamas. The woman on the other side of the door looked just like Jackie, a little darker and without the up turned nose, but it wasn't hard to tell they were related. Her black hair was in a perfect chignon, and she was dressed in a pristine gray suit. Slowly, I blinked myself into the moment. "Are you here for Jackie?"

"Yes, of course. It is time to go to church. It is Sunday," she said with the insinuation that I should really considering joining.

"Right, let me go tell her you're here." I was about to shut her out when the belated light bulb turned on. "Do you want to wait inside?"

Her cold eyes held a mocking edge. "Thank you for the offer, but no. I'll wait here. Tell Jacqueline to hurry."

"Of course." Shutting the door, I stumbled back up the stairs. The room to the guest room was opening, and I could hear a few other life forms stirring throughout the house.

"Nora?" asked Jackie, leaning against the door to support herself. "Is that my mother?"

I nodded, sharing her misery.

"Great, where is my bag?" She didn't wait for an answer, padding down the stairs. She fell over one of the other girls, and the ensuing ruckus brought Celeste down as well.

"Is everything alright, girls?" she asked, clutching a dressing gown to her throat.

"Oh, sure, if you consider my mother is here," replied Jackie darkly. "Honestly, it wouldn't kill me to miss one Sunday."

Amber stretched, rubbing sleep from her eyes. "Crap, that means my dad will be by soon, too." She crawled over Lara to get to her bag. It was madness for the next five minutes as they all struggled to get dressed. Celeste and I rolled up sleeping bags, and in less than ten minutes, not only had everyone's parents arrived, they had all been bundled off to Sunday services.

"Whew," sighed Celeste, sitting awkwardly on the sofa. "That was unexpected. Would you like breakfast now?"

"No, I'd really like to just go back to sleep."

She smiled wryly, one hand on her belly rubbing absently. "I completely understand. Unfortunately, your father snores."

"You could take my bed," I said. "I can sleep on a couch."

She shook her head slowly. "No, I'm fine, really."

I stopped at the archway leading to the stairs and turned back. "Don't you go to church?" I asked, remembering that my mother always had.

"Not anymore," she replied with a wry quirk of her lips. "When your own mother shuns you, it doesn't make the experience worthwhile."

"When you marry my dad, will it be better for

you?"

"With my mother? Hardly, but with the rest of the town, probably. My brother will make sure no one shuns me afterwards."

"My mom used to take me."

Her finely groomed eyebrows popped up in surprise. "Really? I just assumed, with your father being the way he is---"

"Oh, my father never went. And after my mom died, neither did I, but, if you'd like, I'd go with you. Even now."

She smiled sadly and shook her head. "Thank you, Nora, that truly means a lot to me, but I made my bed."

"Sometimes," I said carefully, "we make our bed, but we didn't choose the sheets."

She rocked back and laughed. "That was precious, and something I would have said when I was younger. Go, get some sleep, my dear."

A point of fact, it was something she had said when I was a child. At the last possible second, I threw myself from my bed and cracked my window, belatedly remembering that I had to be up to learning to cook today. It hurt to focus on a point so far in my future, and after I managed that, I promptly passed back out.

TEN

"You sleep like the dead."

I jerked up in bed at the sound of Ivan's voice. Realizing who it was, I flopped back down and glared at him. "Good to see you, too."

He just shrugged, and sat at the foot of my bed. "Hey, you said come by. I'm just doing what I'm told."

It was childishly immature, but I couldn't resist sticking my tongue out at him. "Is it already one?"

"Yeah, I thought I'd wait to see if you woke up, but you didn't, so I felt compelled to help."

"Help, right." I rubbed my eyes and tried to remember why I was so miserable. Oh, right, because I hadn't had any sleep. "Alright, I'm up. Just give me a few minutes to get dressed, and I might want to tell Celeste I'm leaving."

"Doesn't that ruin the point of your window?"

I sighed and reluctantly put my feet on the braided rug beside me. "Hey, she's been nice lately. It just doesn't feel right to run off. But if she's asleep, I'll come back. Oh, crap, my dad's back. You're right, just let me get dressed and I'll go."

His eyes narrowed ever so slightly. "You're willing to tell your future step mother, but not your dad?"

"He does it often enough to me, maybe if I take to wandering off without a word he might care enough to tell me when he does the same thing."

He quickly hid his surprise at my tone, getting off the bed. "Well, I'll be in the alley if you need me."

It hurt to have my worst suspicions confirmed. When I stumbled into the bathroom and turned on the light, my hair was a mess and I looked awful. Great, just how I wanted to appear. I had a feeling I had looked just as bad if not worse when Jackie's mom had come. I wanted a shower, but I didn't think Ivan would wait that long. Remembering his suggestions that I not dress too nicely, I donned the jeans I had come into this world in and a nondescript sweater before climbing down after him.

"You weren't kidding," he said, ever so slightly impressed. "When you said you'd be right down, you were right down. Even I take longer to get ready in the morning."

Smiling, I reached out and touched his shiny hair. "Yeah, I can see where that might be a problem for you." I pulled on my pony tail and frowned at it. The waves never went in the same direction and a few liked to sneak out from the top. Hairspray and head bands only did so much. "This, on the other hand, gets worse the more I play with it."

He pulled the hair from my fingers and gave it a playful tug. Even as kids he had liked to play with my hair. Even as kids, I had liked to tease him about his. "It shows personality, now come on. Mom has lunch planned out, and I apparently have to wait for you to cook before I get to eat."

"You could be waiting awhile."

He laughed, pulling me along at a skipping gait. "I know, that's why we need to hurry."

In the daylight, with the October sun crisply shining on even the darkest corner, even the Village looked beautiful. Outside of Shotgun Alley the world looked like a perfect postcard, with the color touched up. Within the battered zone, the pain spoke in low whistles through abandoned windows, and every ounce of life was made more precious because of it. I was again reminded of Edgar Allen Poe, and I half expected a raven on a lamp post. I might hate horror movies, but I did love a subtle thriller.

Ivan let us in without having to ring, and we weren't immediately pounced by his miniatures.

"Where are your brothers?" I asked as I followed him up. Today there were more people in the building. The residents of the first floor all came out to see me. And I was pretty positive that was all they were out for. Ivan didn't even bother to acknowledge them, pushing me ahead of him up the stairs.

"Len is with one of his friends for the day. Ajay and Jorge went down to the park. Sofia offered to feed Ajay earlier and he jumped at the chance."

"They were that frightened of my cooking?"

Trotting around me, he got the door, laughing at me all the time. "No, but they only have weekends at home, so they like to see all of their friends while they're here."

"Why do they only get to see their friends on

weekends?"

He pushed me in as I dawdled. "After what happened to my father, we couldn't find a school near that would take Ajay. I was already in the system, and I had enough friends to be protected, but Ajay was only five. The abuse was unbearable. Most of it was verbal, but it just wasn't something we could make him endure. My aunt lives up outside of Santrope, its about two hours north. They go to school up there and stay with her during the weekdays and come home on Fridays."

"That's horrible," I whispered, my hand at my mouth.

He shrugged, pushing me along to the kitchen. "It's life."

It was on the tip of my tongue to ask why they didn't move, but I remembered Jimmy's description of the watch list. Surely Padma and Ivan were at the top of that list.

"Nora! You made it." Padma hurried to hug me. "Come, I hope you don't mind, I started without you." She handed a plate of egg rolls to her son. "I knew he'd be a pest if I didn't."

"Of course I don't mind," I assured her, stepping aside as Ivan left with his food. She smiled and handed me another plate.

"And I also knew he wouldn't share. Now, I don't know what your favorites are, so I thought we'd start simple."

"Simple sounds good," I replied, closing my eyes in bliss as the fresh egg roll oozed into my mouth. Years of frozen food had left me wanting, and that all became abundantly clear as I finished the tasty treat in two bites. "That was heavenly," I said, handing the plate back.

"You can finish them," she replied with amusement dancing in her dark eyes.

"Oh, no, I'm good."

With an effort, she smoothed the smile from her lips and took the other egg roll for herself. "I will never say a word about what you choose to eat here," she said gently. "Least of all if I made it."

I blushed. "What gave me away?"

She laughed lightly and handed me an apron. "My mother used to do the same to me. Tell me not to eat this, only eat that. My father loved his sweets, and while she couldn't keep him from eating junk, she decided to keep me and my sisters healthy."

I came to stand beside her, noticing the array of food spread out before me. "What don't you know how to cook?" I asked in wonder.

"Very little," she replied with a laugh. "My mother was from India, and she loved true Indian cuisine, but my father loved his bangers and mash, and begged for treacle tart. When I married Ivan's father, he came from just as diverse a back ground. His father was from Madrid and loved tapas, his mother was from Kiev and loved piroshki. I learned to make just about anything. Irena taught me to make her family recipe for borscht, among other things, so I have family recipes for three nationalities. Other than that, I tend to rely on a cook book."

"So, Spanish, Hindi, Ukrainian, and English? That explains the languages Ivan knows."

"Oh that isn't all of them. He worked really hard to learn a little of every language he comes into contact with. Especially those who helped after."

"That's impressive. I managed to get through three years of Spanish in class, but that's all I've ever got."

"Didn't you pick up anything when you traveled?"

"Not so much. I don't have the talent for languages like Ivan does."

"Neither do I. Now, let's get started. We're going to be making chicken tacos. It's pretty straight forward. We'll progress to chicken curry and something like Kung Pao later."

I followed her every movement, helping to start the chicken as she told me about the heat of the burner and the seasonings. "How did Sofia manage all that food after hours?" I asked. "I thought the power was shut off."

"Most of us have an old fashioned system to fall back on. Some go so far back as a fire, some of the more industrious have figured out how to run a smaller oven off of batteries and propane. I prefer to have my cooking done before the power is cut. I've never trusted those methods. Especially not after I singed my eyebrows starting Mimi's contraption two years ago. I know I was lucky to get away so unscathed, but it's scarred me."

"I can imagine. I get nervous with my oven."

She chuckled, and I thought I had to be doing her a fair amount of good. After all, laughter was like chocolate and released happy endorphins. Padma didn't spare me, either. I was not sent to chop the vegetables and basically relegated to nothing. I was kept by the burners, making fresh tortillas and keeping an eye on the chicken while she did the chopping. Some of those tortillas didn't turn out so well, but she had been expecting this, making a double batch of the dough. When all was said and done, she helped me put the food on plates, but they started being moved on their own. Padma finished the plate with the toppings only to have it vanish. Ivan came in and did the same for the chicken, beans, and tortillas. She just rolled her eyes and untied her apron.

"Teenage boys," she said with long suffering patience. "The worst part is, in another thirty minutes he'll be hungry again. We need to hurry, or there won't be anything left."

To my surprise, Ivan ate with manners. And there was enough left over for Padma and me to eat healthy portions.

"So, what have you been doing with your time?" asked Padma.

"Well, some classmates came over yesterday for movies. Their parents didn't seem too thrilled when they came to get them for church this morning."

Ivan paused mid bite and stared hard at me. "Who?"

"Jackie, Amber, Lara, and Krystal."

He dropped his food back to the plate and even Padma stopped eating.

"And how was it?" asked Padma politely, glaring at her son.

"Fine, I guess. We watched horror movies, I don't do horror movies, but after the others fell asleep, Jackie and I watched a few Disney flicks. I think Celeste even enjoyed herself. She made three separate platters for us. Of course, her idea of food and mine are very different."

"No doubt," replied Padma with a small smile. "Well, I'm sure it is good for you to be making friends."

"I wouldn't call them friends," I said, picking at the pieces on my plate. "They're very cliquey. But Jackie didn't seem so bad."

Ivan pushed back his chair and pivoted towards the kitchen. Padma sighed and pushed her plate aside.

"He doesn't deal well with that family," she said, and I was further chastised by the rebuke in her words.

"I can totally understand, but I'm not asking him to be friends with them."

"Aren't you?"

"No, my best friend back home, he was friends with half the school. He was my only friend. People here actually seem interested in knowing me."

She smiled tightly and began to gather dishes.

"I think Jackie and I have something in common," I said quietly.

Padma stopped and turned back to me. "What is that?" she asked, doubt evident in her voice.

I slowly turned to look at her. "Her parents ignore her. From the way she talks about it, she sees them about as much as I see my dad. No one should be held responsible for their parents."

"No," she said, her voice catching. "But they are."

"Well," I got up and brought the rest of the plates to the kitchen. "If you need help cleaning, I can learn that too."

"Thank you, Nora, but I'm alright."

"I think I can make my way home. If not, maybe I'll run into Jimmy or Maria. I'm so sorry," I said, not a hundred percent sure what I was apologizing for.

She took the plates from my hands and smiled reassuringly at me. "I know you don't mean to upset any of us. You're a sweetheart, Nora."

"No I'm not. I'm a brat. If you don't want me back next week, I understand."

"Why wouldn't I? Don't be foolish, dear. I enjoyed your company today. These are my only days off, and, unlike my son, I won't hold what you do with your time against you."

"Thanks, for everything."

"If you want to wait, I can see you home. I need to get a hold of Sofia first."

"No, I really think I can make it back. Something I learned to do really early in life was find my way back. I wasn't guaranteed to have anyone follow."

A flash of pity appeared in her eyes, but she didn't say anything. I let myself out, wallowing in self pity. At the corner of the street, I took a moment to think back to my previous trips. Sighing, I turned left and began my way back home.

"You are an idiot," said a sharp voice behind me.

"Did I go the wrong direction?" I asked caustically.

"No, but you shouldn't go alone."

"I didn't want to make things difficult for your mother."

"Again, you are an idiot."

"Shut up," my voice cracked and I really wanted him to leave me alone.

"Hold up, Princess," he pulled me around to face him. Even though I was facing him didn't mean I had to look at him. I dropped my gaze to my feet.

"What do you want?"

"Look, I'm sorry," he said, and I had to glance up. He was clearly struggling with the concept of an apology. "It's none of my business who you hang out with."

"It is," I replied quietly. "You're my best friend."

"The other me is your best friend."

"No, the other you was. I don't know what I'd do without you, in this world or any other. I'm sorry you don't appreciate that I can be social with Jackie in this world. In the other you would have been in alt."

"In the other, I'm the idiot, not you." His lips twitched, and he guided me back along the street. "I was an ass, and I apologize."

"Did your mother yell at you?"

"My mother never yells."

I snorted. "That says a lot."

He sighed in frustration. "I would have apologized eventually."

"She just forced the issue."

"Maybe. And you're right, I shouldn't judge Jackie just because her father single handedly destroyed my family."

"He single handedly destroyed my life in the other world, if that helps."

"Not really. But, hey, misery loves company, right?"

"Right." We crossed two more streets before I spoke again. "You know, I don't think you should let Jackie know about your new found open-mindedness."

"Who said anything about being open minded?"

"You did."

"What? Oh, you interpreted what I said to be open mindedness." He tweaked my hair. "Please don't put words in my mouth."

"Is that even possible?"

"No, not really," but he laughed all the same. "So why don't I want to let Jackie know I might be open to the idea of not hating her?"

"I think, ironically, she has a crush on you."

He tipped his head back and laughed loud enough to have strangers stare at us. "That is ironic. Alright, I promise not to give myself away."

"Ivan! Nora!" we turned to see Jimmy trotting up to us.

"Hey, Jimmy," I said with a smile.

"Hey, glad I caught you. I meant to give this to you on your birthday, Nora, but I didn't have the metal perfectly set in time." He handed over a necklace, with a beautifully designed encasing around my piece of mirror.

"Oh, Jimmy, it's beautiful." I turned it over in amazement. "You have a gift."

He shrugged. "Sometimes. So, what are you doing on this end of town?"

"Mrs. Battuta is teaching me to cook."

Pointedly, Jimmy looked between the two of us. "Really?"

"Oh, give off," said Ivan with exaggerated annoyance. "Isn't it possible Nora could genuinely want to know how to cook something more than macaroni and cheese?"

"I've never made macaroni and cheese," I said helpfully. "I managed to burn some toast the other day, but I blame the oven on that. I couldn't find a toaster."

Jimmy's eyes widened. "Seriously, you don't know how to make toast?"

"Like I said, if I knew where the toaster was, I'd have been fine. And I can manage instant oatmeal, T.V. dinners, and Pop Tarts."

Jimmy let out a low whistle. "Dang girl, I can cook more than you can. No wonder you need help."

"Oh, that's comforting, thank you."

He laughed and ruffled my hair. "Any time. You two still set on going out to the island tomorrow?" he asked, turning instantly sober.

"Of course," I replied, surprised to even be asked.

"Well, I'll go over tomorrow, then, meet me at the docks. I checked the schedule, the late shift ferry leaves at five, and comes back at one. It'll be a rough ride home."

Ivan nodded, understanding the danger better than me. "Any buses back to Walnut at that hour?"

Jimmy nodded. "One, but you'll have to run to make the interchange. And the drivers up north of Merry are pretty pretentious." He looked hard at me, assessing my qualities I suppose. At least he didn't find me wanting. "You'll have to rely on her to get you back to our end. There are no buses deeper than Walnut. The unlucky few who get off at that time are expected to walk or live closer to the island."

"Thanks, I'll make sure to go over the transit times. I think they make it difficult to try and shut those businesses down."

"No doubt. If I thought it would work, I'd try

to get you to reconsider, but I know you won't." he sighed, looking between the two of us. "I know a few people who work out there. I might be able to get you a guide."

"One who wouldn't hate me?"

"You could always try cutting your hair."

"You're just saying that to get me to do it. Any excuse."

"Maybe." He shook his head at Ivan. Giving him up as a lost cause, he looked to me. "You'll need to layer up, Nora. It'll be best if anyone who sees you can see you're from the good side of town."

I frowned at him. "How is it everyone knows where I come from? There are enough ethnicities here, it would be impossible to tell."

"Nah, you stand out. There's no one thing to tell you. Just make sure you have some designer label thing on when you get back. But not when you go over."

"So pack extra?"

"Something like that, yeah." He just shook his head at Ivan. "If that's a definite no on the hair, then you'll just have to hope no one recognizes you now. And stay with her when you're on Walnut."

"You sound worse than my mother."

"Ivan, I'm not kidding. That island is a piece of work. And so is anyone stubborn enough to stay out there. And you and I both know what the cops are like towards us. They know you, and they know me. We're not safe after hours. Least of all you."

"Thanks for the help, we'll see you at the docks," said Ivan, taking me by the hand and leading us on. I turned and waved over my shoulder. He just stood there shaking his head at us.

"Thank you, by the way," I said as we crossed into the safe zone.

"For what?" he asked, dropping my hand, acting as though he had just realized he was holding it.

"For not trying to make me stay home."

"You wouldn't listen."

"That wouldn't stop Jimmy."

"It didn't stop Jimmy. And now he'll start thinking you're a bad influence on me. Too bad for you, he was starting to like you."

"Is it really as dangerous as he made it sound?'

Ivan shrugged. "Depends. The city stops at the harbor. Any police intervention stops there."

"But the police don't seem that impartial."

"They're not, at least not where the Village is concerned, and anyone related to me."

"Are you sure you're safe?"

"Don't even think about trying that track, Princess. If I don't go, you don't. And I thought it was important to find this maker."

"It is. I don't trust my father to look too hard for his mother. He told me he had asked for a few favors, but he wouldn't look at me when he said it. He's up to something, and he and his mother have hated each other as long as I can remember, but especially since my mom died. If Grandmère found out about Celeste," I shivered, "I could definitely see him leaving her to her own problems."

"Well, we should be fine on the crossing, if things are really bad, Jimmy will tell us before we try. If not, as long as we stay under the radar, we should be able to slip anywhere we want and not be noticed. It'll only be a problem if someone sees us. Let me correct that, it's only a problem if someone sees us and either recognizes me or recognizes you."

"No one is going to recognize me."

"Not exactly, no, but Jimmy's right. There's just something about you that doesn't fit this world. It makes you unique, but here, anyone who doesn't blend is a threat."

"Of course I don't fit in this world, I'm not from it."

"No, it's something more. I can't put a finger on what, but it's there. Those of us from the Village, we just see that a little bit more than anyone outside. Out there, if you're different, it could be okay. In the Village, if you're different, you could be a threat and a traitor. I'd suggest a hat, and as nondescript a coat as you have."

"I can manage that. What am I supposed to do about coming home, though?"

"Besides losing the hat? I think we'll just have to wing it. We can't carry another outfit for you, and it'll be freezing. The bus stops about three blocks north of where you live. We should be fine."

"Should be?"

"Should be."

It was not the most resounding endorsement of a course of action, but I had to take it. No matter what happened, I needed to try and find my grandmother. I couldn't very well rely on my father to do so. I hadn't been able to rely on him to do anything in years.

ELEVEN

No one had even noticed I was missing. This was pretty par for course, but it still bothered me. However, Celeste, in her defense, had been sleeping and thought I just needed the rest after the night before.

Now, I had ample time to watch my father and the woman who was almost my mother. For a man who never hugged me, it burned a hole in my stomach to see how he stayed so close to her, keeping a hand on or near her no matter where they were. He didn't seem to show all that much interest in his second child either, though, and petty though it might be, that made me feel a tiny bit better. To say that dinner was an awkward affair would be like saying the Titanic was unsinkable. I was too angry to be civil, and my father was too craven to try and talk me down. Celeste didn't know how to mediate between us, and so we ate predominantly in silence. When the meal was finished, my father called me into the living room when I would have been helping Celeste clean up.

"Nora, this has got to stop," he said by way of an introduction.

"What would that be?" I asked with false cheeriness.

"You know what I mean. Look, I know I wasn't a perfect father, but you can't just shut us down."

"Technically speaking, you still aren't a perfect father, there is no past tense."

"Nora."

"What?" I could feel the rage, and I tried to breath through it, but I couldn't stop it. "You w-want me t-t-o g-g-give you a free p-pass? When hell f-freezes over."

"You still stutter?" he asked in surprise.

"Obviously."

"I had no idea."

"That's no surp-prise."

"Nora, please. Can we try for a civil conversation?"

"No."

"Can we try for any conversation?"

Reminding myself I was only seventeen, I heaved a sigh and flopped onto one of the arm chairs. "I am not unwilling to listen."

"What do you want to know?"

"A lot." I counted to ten, trying to control my temper and my tongue. I had to speak slowly when I was so worked up or I couldn't talk at all. "Why did you leave to find Celeste?"

"What is the purpose of being a World Walker if I couldn't be with the woman I love?"

"She isn't my mother."

"No, I know that, but she's the closest there is."

"Did you look in every world?"

"Most, yes."

"And that's it? You k-kept looking f-f-for her?" I paused, biting my tongue and giving my words a chance to catch up, "Rather than stay with me?"

"I hadn't thought it would be so difficult. I wanted you to have your mother too, Nora. I thought we could start again. But then after I found Celeste here, I started being tracked in several of the other worlds. It wasn't safe for me to stay anywhere. I wanted us to start fresh then, but I had to try and get a few things settled first. I was going to come for you, with the plan that we leave after Ivan did."

That brought my self pity up short. "What did you just say?"

He flushed, pulling his hand down his face in agitation. "I knew you wouldn't want to leave while Ivan was there. Despite what you might think, I knew about him in this realm. My mother especially did, more than you know, and so I suspected what he might mean in the other. I pulled a few strings there to get his dad a promotion. Ideally we would have moved when he did, and it would have been a natural parting."

"I can't believe you," I whispered in agony. "You bastard! You had n-no r-right!"

"I am your father, I had every right!"

"W-what ab-bout me? T-that was my life!"

"You're a World Walker, Nora, you can have a life anywhere. And here, Celeste tells me you're already settling in, and you've found Ivan. What more do you want?"

"To be asked. Jus-just once, Dad." I got up, ready to bolt.

"I can take you back, if that's what you really want, but not until I finish a few things. If you truly want to go back to the Twelfth Realm, I'll take you, just give me a few more days."

"Would you be coming?"

"No."

"Then it's not really an option." I ran to my room, praying he let me be after that. I wanted to run from the house, run for the safety of Ivan and Padma, but I saw the full moon rising, and knew it was too late. Instead, I took a shower, crying the whole time, and finally fell into a fitful sleep. Now, in addition to the horror of chainsaws, I had to contend with my father's betrayal in my dreams.

I was paler and more drawn than was usual even for me when I met up with Ivan and Maria at the bus station.

"Hey, Nora," said Maria. "How was your weekend?"

I frowned at her, trying to figure out how to answer that. "It was eventful," I finally settled with.

"A couple of friends and I are going to the movies next weekend," she said with a charming smile. "Do you want to come?"

"Sure, I'd like that."

"Cool, I'll let you know what movie we settle on."

"Please not horror."

She laughed. "I see you've met Amber. No, since it'll just be girls, we'll probably settle for a rom-com. Otherwise known as a chick flick, but don't worry, I'll let you know."

"Thanks."

"No problem. You know, you look a little peaked."

"I don't sleep well after horror movies."

She nodded. "Totally understand. I was given the dubious honor of being Amber's lab partner last year. She invited me over a couple times, that is until her parents figured out where I came from. I still have nightmares."

"There must be something wrong with her psyche to enjoy them."

"Nah, all my brothers do. They got chewed out royally by my dad when he and my mom found out that they were pulling pranks when I couldn't sleep."

"No offense, but I think that means your brothers have issues too."

She laughed. "You're probably right."

I was surprised when a coffee cup was pressed into my hand. I smiled gratefully at Jimmy.

"You'll need this," he said. "And tell Ivan to get you some on the way back tonight too."

"You're an angel," I replied, taking a sip.

"Don't thank me, it was his idea," he said, tipping his head towards Ivan.

"What about me?" asked Maria.

Jimmy handed over another cup. "You're so demanding."

"Don't you know it?" she replied cheekily, taking a sip. "Thank you Ivan!"

"No, that one was me," Jimmy replied wryly. "Honestly, your lack of gratitude is heart breaking."

She made a face at him and was the first to load up as the bus pulled to a stop. Jimmy grinned at me as he waited for me to go ahead. "Actually, Ivan got it for her too, but I don't want her getting the wrong idea."

"Wrong idea?" I asked, making my way to the

back.

"No sense in her trying to genuinely thank him, he wouldn't do it again if she tried."

"But now she'll expect it from you."

"Nah, she knows better. I need to go to the front. It'll be a mad dash to make my transfer on time. Please, feel free to change your mind and let me know tonight."

"I won't."

"Didn't think so. See you later, Nora."

"Bye, Jimmy."

Ivan finally migrated back to me as the bus started to move. "Last ditch effort?" he asked, taking the surprisingly available seat.

"Something like that."'

"He thinks you're the weak link. Little does he know."

"Thanks for the coffee."

"You looked liked you needed it."

"Jimmy suggested we get some on our way out tonight."

"We can try, but I don't think we'll manage. Maybe they'll have one of those vending machine versions on the ferry. Besides, the problem will come around one in the morning, not five in the evening."

"Thank you," I said, squeezing his hand.

"Don't thank me yet," he replied, carefully extracting his hand and glowering at the boys who were watching us.

"Well, if I don't thank you now, and we die or are arrested, when am I supposed to?"

"In the squad car, that would be pretty poetic. Stop worrying, and stop talking about it. We should really teach you something other than

English." He looked up and down the bus. "Might try for Russian, it looks like the least common language on this bus."

"Are we starting now?"

"No, you need something to look forward to after tonight. Besides, if we're really lucky, maybe we'd have neighboring cells while they processed us."

I laughed, he was being deliberately outrageous, but it helped ease the growing terror of the unknown.

School was agony. It was impossible to focus on anything, and with my new found popularity, I was being stressed by more than just class work. I settled for smiling and nodding my head to any question. I was too wound up to manage complete sentences unless it had been Ivan I was answering them to. Ivan took no chances, hunting me down after class and pulling me along for the bus. Brad and Maria took our bags without question at the first interchange.

"How is this going to work?"

"Chances are you won't be turning the homework in on time," he replied.

"So, we get our stuff back tomorrow?"

"That's the plan. Come on, we need to run."

It was crazy, but four buses later, we were at the pier watching the ferry come in. Jimmy was one of the first off, looking a little frazzled himself.

"Its not as bad as I thought," he said. "But it's sure not any better than it was. Go on, the operators are about as social as security guards at a packed concert. Ivan," he grabbed a hold of Ivan's arm and pulled him aside. I had to wait, growing increasingly nervous as the rest of the passengers

filed on. I stood out, and that's putting it lightly.
Coming back to me, Ivan pulled me along. When
we were on board, he took me down into the hold,
hiding us both behind one of the support beams
and cargo crates.

"What did Jimmy say?" I asked.

"Nothing much. Stay close when we get off.
He gave me a crude map on where to go, but we'll
need to get there quickly."

I nodded in apprehensive agreement. It wasn't
as if I had seen myself taking a whole bunch of
pictures and taking in the ambiance. The
announcement of arrival came in three languages,
but Ivan didn't need to wait for the third before
pulling me up. We slipped between the masses
and off the ship without any incident. Looking up,
I felt my heart lurch down, down, down. We had
landed on a little piece of hell.

Fires from the two remaining factories flared in
harsh bursts like on an oil rig. Two buildings were
obviously in service, but another dozen or so
weren't. Chain link fences surrounded a few, with
rolls of barbed wire. At the top of the island sat a
garrison with a search light running a sort of patrol.
Workers pushed past on their way to their site.
Ivan grabbed my hand and led me off the beaten
path, through a chunk of cut fencing, past a rubbish
pile the size of my house, and finally down a
deserted alley. The moon filtered through, making
the buildings shine back where they still had
windows. The search light ran consistent passes,
but could hardly penetrate through the
surrounding structures. I couldn't come up with
how this place was supposed to be more beautiful
than anywhere in my world. If anything, all the

hideousness that was absent on the main land had accumulated here. It was like a horror version of the *Dark Knight's* Gotham City. Ivan stopped and angled the map every which way before figuring out where the next turn was, taking up my hand again and pulling me deeper into this cess pit. At the base of the garrison were four more functioning buildings. To one side was what looked like an after thought. It was a quarter of the size, but with twice the protection. Ivan abandoned me in the safety of a stack of crates before going off on a reconnaissance mission. He came back and without another word, led me in.

There was a padlock on the back door, and it was the least secured entrance. Ivan examined it for a good minute before pulling out tools he had once shown me and making quick work of the hurdle before us. The chains crashed down before he could catch them. When he cautiously opened the door, it groaned in protest. He looked back at me in mathematical calculation, forcing it open another three inches before slipping through. I followed, impressed that it had been open just enough for me to fit through after him. We cautiously crept through the near pitch black confines towards the front end. Ivan pulled out a flashlight from his jacket, which he had swapped for his blazer before boarding the bus, and led me by the hand. We had cleared two rooms before he stopped abruptly. Holding a hand to his lips, he tilted his head and strained to hear something. I did too, amazed to hear voices. Before he could tell me what to do, I slipped past, edging closer. As I passed through the room, I rounded a corner, and despite my best intentions, I gasped. There before me was a room full of mirrors. And not just mirrors, but Portals. Each one was set up to form an oval around the room, and by my quick count there were forty one, the exact number of other worlds. The voices had stopped when I gasped, and in my awe struck wonder, I was easy prey. A strong set of hands grabbed hold of me and pushed me into the light.

"What do we have here?" asked a deep, bitter voice.

"Cameron?" asked another.

"We have a trespasser, Grandfather," called out my captor.

"Well, bring him here."

"It's a girl."

"Then bring her here, honestly boy."

I was brought to the very center, where the mirrors reflected the meager light to a near electric point. Blue tinted light bounced off the walls, and I felt like I was in the middle of a prism.

"What are you doing here, child?" asked the other man. He came forward, bent over a cane, but his sharp eyes intent on me.

"I came here for the Portals," I replied.

"What do you know about them?" asked Cameron harshly, pushing me a step further.

"Stop bullying her," snapped his grandfather. He finally got to within a few feet of me, and let out a low whistle. "Good God, you're Alanna's granddaughter."

"You know my grandmother?"

He smiled, his well lined face lighting up. "She's my sister."

TWELVE

All I could do for several drawn out seconds was stare. He had the same purple-gray eyes I did, and I knew that of all my relatives I took after my grandmother the most. Slowly, I turned to look at the person beside me. That would make him my cousin. He was taller than me, with dark blond hair, but he too had my eyes. We stared for several more moments, each of us trying to figure this out.

"Hello, Cousin," I said haltingly.

"Hello," he replied.

"You must be Peter's daughter," said the older man. "It is a pleasure to finally meet you." He extended his hand, and weakly I shook it. "My name is Carl, this is my grandson, Cameron. I take it you inherited the ability to World Walk?"

I nodded, still overwhelmed. Carl smiled broadly and clapped Cameron on the shoulder.

"And here you thought you were the only one. What Realm did you come from?"

"The Twelfth."

"Ah, makes sense. I'm sorry, my dear, but you are, Eleanor?"

"Alinora. Nora for short."

"A pleasure, a pleasure." He bopped his grandson upside his head.

"Nice to meet you," Cameron dutifully uttered.

"Nice to meet you, too," I said dryly. Carl watched me carefully, and then scanned the room.

"Nora, dear, would you do me a favor and call out your companion? He's good, I'll give him that, but I don't relish the idea of being ambushed, and these mirrors are so valuable."

"Ivan?"

He slipped form behind a Portal, frowning at the older man. "How did you figure it out?"

"It was a reflection, dear boy, you are, like I said, very good. Stealth like, but if you're from the Village, I can see why you need to be." Pivoting awkwardly, Carl held out his hand to Ivan. "I am Carl Terre."

"Ivan Battuta."

The old man's face sparked with surprise. "Lenin's son?"

Ivan nodded, edging closer to me. Carl looked between Ivan and me over and over again. "How long have you known each other?" he asked, and the sweet old man was gone, replaced by a sharp disciplinarian.

"About ten years," I replied, taking Ivan's hand when he was close enough to grab.

"Ah, that explains it. And this Ivan? Not one from another world?"

"Yes, this one."

He nodded, but his shrewd eyes continued to watch Ivan closely.

"What?" asked Cameron for all of us.

"Later, first I'd like to know what you're doing

here. You were brave to venture so deep into the island. It's part of the reason I relocated here. No one asks questions out here."

"Grandmère went missing," I said. "She left me a note asking to have my father come after her, and a piece of the Portal she was stuck behind." I pulled the necklace out from under my blouse, handing it over.

"I had begun to wonder," Carl said, more to himself than the rest of us. He put his cane around his arm and adjusted the lens of his bifocals to read what was on the back of the mirror. "Well, that's interesting. This mirror was made here, but not by me, and it's too old to be Cameron's work." He turned the shard in his hand. "What happened when you bled on it?"

"It showed another world. One like out of the end of the *Lord of the Rings*, you know where Hobbiton is overtaken by industry? Only everyone wore shoes and wasn't three feet tall."

Cameron covered a chuckle, but Carl ignored his grandson. I highly doubted Carl even knew what I was talking about. I was rather surprised, given what difference existed here, that Cameron did. "And it's in the thirties. Come my dear," he gestured towards the end of the oval. Each frame had an engraved number atop it. We stopped outside of thirty four. "Give me your hand, Nora."

Even though I knew what was coming, I winced as he took out a pocket knife and sliced open a cut down the pad of my thumb. Holding my hand to the mirror, we all watched as the world began to flash by. After a minute, he let me go.

"Was that it?"

"No," I replied, sucking on my finger

reproachfully.

"Try everything past this. These worlds are similar, except thirty seven, don't bother with that one."

Frowning, I did as he instructed. I was about to give up hope when I put my still bleeding thumb on the thirty ninth mirror. As it began to flash through, Ivan sucked in his breath, and I knew we had found the right place.

"That's it," I said.

"I was afraid of that," he replied, handing me back my necklace. "One of the worst of the Thirty Realms. Last time I dared, it was overrun by two warring clans. I couldn't get off the continent to see what was going on outside the world."

"Do the Europeans exist?" asked Ivan. "Or did the colonies never happen?'

"Oh, they happened, but World War II went horribly wrong in this world, and the people reverted back to near cave like living. They've managed to progress relatively quickly, but technology does not exist there except in pockets. Roads have been left to nature, cities are abandoned, those that survived. The population is a fraction of what it was then, let alone today. And the people have adopted an almost tribal mentality, the feudal system is alive and well, but in recent years, the cities have started to regrow. The war is on between technology and the simplistic. It hasn't been going well."

"But why would Grandmère go there?"

"Alanna has a very different philosophy than most World Walkers. Most of us are observers only, but Alanna tries to help people from time to time," he glanced at Ivan and then back at me. "If we change too much, we inadvertently create a new world. Once, long ago, there were only three. One, of course, where humanity had never come to exist, one where we never became more than primitive, and the one that we now descend from. The first World Walkers tried to change their history, prevent atrocities, the like, and in changing the course of history, they changed their world to the point that the fabric of its creation wove another instead. Alanna is usually very good at minute changes, but she has created one new world. Nearly a second, but she managed to correct that one in time."

"So she's trying to save that world?"

"More likely a single person. I can't tell you why, there are far more mirrors than this. This is just my personal collection. And this is where I am teaching Cameron the craft. I imagine you will soon be coming into your own as well. If you stay in this world, I would happily teach you to create more."

I looked around at the mirrors, astounded and a little proud. This was my heritage staring right back at me. I had never seen it before. Not like this.

"I'd like that," I said.

"Good, now, if you don't mind me asking, why hasn't Peter gone after his mother? I presume you showed him the mirror?"

"Sort of. My father is preoccupied."

Carl's eyes narrowed. "Peter is often preoccupied. I can't believe there is anything more important than his mother's safety."

"Of course there is," I replied, trying hard to keep the bitterness out but failing. "There is

Celeste."

"Your mother? I thought she died."

"She did, in my world. The day before my twelfth birthday."

Carl sucked in breath through his teeth. "Your father is a fool. A besotted fool. Well, I can't very well go through there. I am too much a cripple now, but Cameron can. I warn you, it is dangerous. No one can be trusted," his gaze flickered to Ivan and back. "No matter what they look like."

"I can handle it, Grandpa," said Cameron slightly belligerently.

"Of course." He frowned at me without uttering a word for a full sixty seconds. "How much have you World Walked?"

"This was my first since I was twelve. My father broke my Portal."

Carl let out a string of muttered obscenities. "The things I could say right now, but out of respect, he is your father. Alright, you'll need clothes." He took my finger and forced the wound open again and pressed the wound to the window. He watched intently for several moments before abruptly letting me go.

"As I thought. Cameron, we need to find the crates for this world. They haven't changed much in the last ten years." Carl hobbled around the mirrors, leading the way to staked crates that were marked but in no particular order.

"Over here," called Cameron. I managed not to get flattened by a crate top by a matter of inches. Looking up reproachfully, I was promptly covered in clothes. "Try that, cuz, they should fit. Good color for you too."

My answer was muffled by the clothes, but that

was probably a good thing. When I finally freed myself, I managed to get out of the way of more.

"Try those, Ivan," he called before dropping a final pile and coming down with a resounding thud. He looked over Ivan carefully. "Hmm, those might be a little too big. Go on," he shooed us behind another set of crates. I had to edge closer to the opening to see which end was which, dismayed to find I had been thrown a dress. Or at least that's what it looked like. The material was heavy and blue. Feeling incredibly self conscious, I peeled off my school uniform and put the dress on. It was more like a tunic, stopping at my knees, but with long sleeves. I poked around my pile and found a pair of leggings. Luckily, while the people of that time might have gone back in fashion, they still kept buttons and zippers. The shoes were well worn leather boots of a sort, and there was a vest that went along with the whole ensemble. Feeling like I was dressing up for Halloween, I stared at the vest, trying to figure out which side was which. It was laced on the sides, with no real shoulders, just straps, and a whole bunch of hooks and pockets.

"Nora, you dressed?" asked Ivan.

"Sort of." He came around the corner, staring in equal confusion at his.

"Oh, you have the same problem." He held his up. "I don't get it."

"Same here."

Someone sighed with a huge amount of emphasis and took the vest from Ivan's hands. "Honestly, you might be a one dimensional creature, but surely you can figure a vest out."

"No," replied Ivan tightly. "As a matter of fact, I can't."

Cameron shrugged, pulling the vest over in one smooth motion before tightening the laces on either side. He pulled it a little and then refastened one of the shoulder straps. Ivan looked about ready to deck my cousin, and I didn't blame him.

"There, all set. Now, the hooks are for things like rope, twine, flash lights. The pockets, they usually hold some first aid. This is your life vest, for lack of a better phrase. Where we're going, if you don't wear one, you can get locked up. Only city folk don't bother with a few survival skills. Now, Cousin," he took mine and I was subjected to the same thing Ivan had been, but with a bust line. He tightened the ties so fast, it pulled the breath out of me.

"It's a fashion statement," he said as he gave another little tug. "They're a little like corsets on the ladies. And you're lucky. If you were bone thin, they'd also distrust you. Especially this time of year."

"Oh, thanks," I said sarcastically.

"It wasn't an insult," he said in surprise. "For centuries, humans used the curvaceous body as a symbol of beauty. If you had a few curves, you were likely to survive a brutal winter. Now-a-days, with all the dieting and super models, it's a lost art, but it wasn't an insult." He moved away from further conflict. "Come on, we should probably be going. It'll take awhile to locate where she might be, and time is the same there. Travel after dark is dangerous."

"Same as it is here," I replied dryly.

"Exactly."

Carl was standing in front of the mirror with a few last minute additions. "Here, it's a map, keep it close. Its outdated, of course, but it should get you back here if you need to. And a few necessities," he handed Ivan and me little travel first aid packs while Cameron attached a few other tools to our vests. The items that dangled had another leather strap to hold them in place. By the time they were both done, I felt like a walking tool belt. However, the placement was definitely thought out. The tool-of-all-trades, a pliers/scissors apparatus was to my right, the flashlight to my left, a compass dangling a little below and on my hip, and a small flask of water on my other hip. Everything stayed when I moved, and the central pocket fit the map and the first aid kit. In spite of everything, I was impressed.

"Nora," said Carl quietly. "When you get there, you'll need to use your piece of the Portal to find where Alana is. The closer you get, the more clear the picture will become, but be careful not to bleed on it. This world is deeply distrustful of anything out of the ordinary. I can't imagine what she was doing there. If you're not back in the morning, I'll call for reinforcements."

I nodded. "Thank you."

"Take care of yourself."

I nodded and taking Ivan's hand, we walked through and into the Thirty Ninth Realm. Cameron quickly followed. He put a stake with a yellow tip to one side of the mirror to mark it and then headed off. I started to follow but the most astounding sound stopped me. Turning back, I realized someone else had crossed.

"Jackie?" I asked, totally dumbfounded.

She picked herself up from the ground and dusted off her knees. "Hey. Wow, where are we?"

"What on earth are you doing here?" I asked.

"Following you, obviously."

"Jackie, go back, please."

She crossed her arms and hiked off after Cameron, who had not stopped to see what the commotion was. "No."

I turned to Ivan, but he just shrugged. "I don't think I can get through on my own, so I couldn't throw her through."

"How did she get through?" I asked, knowing it was rhetorical.

Up ahead, Cameron had finally stopped and was swearing at Jackie. "You have to go back. I don't know who you are, but you need to be leaving."

"I don't know who you are," she retorted, "but no."

"Nora!"

"What?"

"Who is she and what is she doing here?"

"Her name is Jackie, and I haven't the slightest idea."

Jackie sighed heavily and glared at us all in equal measure. "I heard you and Ivan talking about coming to Finch Island. No one comes here without a really good reason, and so I followed you after school. It was hard to keep up with you on the island itself, but I made it just in time. The old man tried to grab me, but I made it through."

"That old man," said Cameron through clenched teeth, "is my grandfather."

"Oh, really? What is all of this? I've never seen anything like it."

Cameron just looked at me incredulously. "You were followed?"

"Right, like I could do something about that!" I cried.

"He could have. Honestly, someone from the Village should have more common sense."

"What is that supposed to mean?" asked Ivan levelly.

"You know what it means," replied Cameron.

"No, I don't."

"Can we focus?" I asked, my voice cracking on its octave. "How do we get her back?"

"One of has to go back through," replied Cameron. "We open the Portal, and they usually stay open for a minute or two after we pass. That's why we are always so careful."

"Your mirror," I replied sharply.

"Your friend," he rejoined.

Ivan clapped a hand over my mouth before I could argue. Cameron turned around, hearing the noise and swore again. "Come on," he said in a fierce whisper. "We need to hide." Leading the charge, we sprinted down a hill, finding an outcropping of trees. Cameron kept pushing on, pulling Jackie along with him until we were deep in the forest. From the distance, I could hear the sound of hooves. At the base of the forest, we could just make out the crest of the hill we had descended. Five riders came over it at warp speed. One spun his horse around, and it nearly fell on the wet grass, but he steadied it and called out to the others. In another moment, a dozen more riders had joined them, and I felt my stomach drop at the sound of baying hounds. I had never personally witnessed a hunt, but I had a feeling I was going to get some personal experience. Cameron pulled Jackie on, and Ivan and I followed. I tried to watch the horses and run at the same time, but tripped over a tree root. Ivan picked me up, and we hurried on. Finally, we ran into a stream bed. Cameron hurried back towards the horses on the path. I wanted to question the reasonableness of this action, but I didn't dare speak. Instead, we splashed upstream until we came to an outcrop of boulders. Unceremoniously, Cameron pushed Jackie down, crouching over her to hide her from view. Ivan and I hid behind a singularly massive boulder, and we all waited even as the pounding hooves grew louder. I didn't dare move, but they got so close I could start to make out their voices. One horse nickered and another snorted, and I could tell they were mere feet from our position. The dogs, however, had caught our scent where we entered the water, and were barking back down stream.

"They've gone to water," cried one of the riders. "Follow them!" They went charging off after the dogs and it was a good five minutes before I felt comfortable enough to breathe again.

"What just happened?" I asked breathlessly.

"Hunting parties. They patrol the boarders. Usually they're looking for runaways or spies from another clan or from the cities. Someone must be around here and we distracted the dogs."

"Good idea to go towards them," said Ivan, helping me to my feet.

"Yeah, they aren't the deepest thinking group of people. Sometimes it's safest to hide in their shadow."

"Wh-what j-just happened?" chattered Jackie.

"You were just saved from something you had no business being in," replied Cameron coldly.

"Crap, you're going to freeze. Come on, there should be a house nearby. If we're really lucky, no one will be home."

Seeking some comfort in the chaos, I reached out and found Ivan's hand. We followed closely, and no one dared say a word. Cameron was right. We came upon a small group of old town houses. The trees had reclaimed most of the surrounding buildings, but a cluster survived. There were a couple children out playing and they all alerted on us. Cameron kept Jackie directly behind him as we approached. An adult had been fetched on our approach.

"What do you want?" asked the roughly hewn woman.

"Clothes, if you have them," replied Cameron. He pulled a few coins from one of his pockets and held them out. "Please."

She frowned at the money and looked at the rest of us. "You don't look like you need clothes to me."

Cameron sighed and pulled Jackie around to stand in front of him. "She does."

The woman jumped as though someone had pinched her. She approached Jackie and tentatively touched her uniform. "Where did you get this?"

"It's my uniform," replied Jackie nervously.

"For what?" asked the woman. "I've never seen anything like it."

"You don't want to know," replied Cameron with a long suffering sigh. "She is trying to leave it all behind, but they took the rest of her clothes. She ran away in this."

"Oh, you poor thing, come, we have a fire going, and dinner should be ready in an hour."

Jackie tried to protest, but Cameron pushed her on. I left Ivan to hurry after her. "Where do you come from?" asked the woman as she led Jackie into one of the houses.

"Santa Rosa," I replied.

"Never heard of it," replied the woman.

"It's pretty far away."

"And you came all this way in that? It's a wonder you didn't' freeze my dear. Don't worry, I think we have a girl here about your size."

Within fifteen minutes, Jackie was dressed and ready, but her look of terror hadn't left. I pulled her back to the fire outside and put her near it so she could warm up, as her lips were still blue.

"Where are we?" she whispered.

"In another world," I replied. "It would have been easier if you hadn't followed."

"I was curious," she replied, clenching her teeth to control the chatter. "You blew me off in History, I couldn't figure it out, then you and Ivan headed this way."

"That's like stalking," I replied, but my lips were twitching. "Are you ready for the whole story?"

"What choice do I have?" she replied.

"Probably none. Look, there are different worlds, a few of us can move between them. I come from another world, not yours, and I'm here because somewhere in this place is my grandmother."

"Oh, can you lie to me and tell me I'll wake up in the morning and forget all this?"

"Sure, Jackie, you'll wake up in the morning with a massive headache and forget all of this."

"Okay, I can handle that."

"But if you want to know more, just ask."

She nodded. "That won't be soon." But not a minute later she was tapping my arm to get my attention. "So how do you know Ivan then?"

"I used to come to your world to play with him as a kid."

"Oh. Okay. But why did you come through this time?"

"I had to."

"Why?"

"Because another Ivan had told another Jackie about my secret and her father wanted to capture me and my father."

"Oh," she chewed on that. "Well, at least I don't need to pine for another father in another world. My dad is an equal opportunity bastard."

I nearly choked, and she had to pat my back to clear my throat.

"You and I, despite all this, have a lot in common," she said. "My dad abandoned me to nannies when I was born. Yours, well, you didn't say what he did exactly. Did it have something to do with this?"

"Sort of."

"Then, like I said." And she nodded for emphasis.

"You're taking this really well."

She sat a little straighter and tossed her head. "How well did Ivan take it?"

"Pretty good. He's here."

"Then I can do no less."

"But you just met me."

She patted my arm. "I don't know, but I think we're going to be friends for a long time, Nora, despite all this. Or maybe because of it. So, who is he?" she asked gesturing towards Cameron.

"He's my cousin, his name's Cameron."

"He's cute," she replied. "And you're related, so I don't need to be jealous." She hopped to her feet. "Wish me luck."

My jaw dropped as she marched off towards an unsuspecting Cameron. Well, not marched per se, it was more sort of a sashay.

"I think I should be relieved," said Ivan, taking the seat she had vacated. "I do believe I am officially free of her sights."

"You didn't hold back on your dislike," I replied. "Just imagine what it could have been."

"I'd rather not, thank you."

"Ah, but it's fun."

He rolled his eyes. "Maybe for you. I have to admit, I'm impressed. She followed us and I didn't notice. Not only that but she gets thrown in here and she's managing to keep up. I would not have expected half as much from her."

"Yeah, I'm impressed too, but heaven help us if we run into her father."

Cameron came back over to us, sweat beading on his forehead. "She's insane," he muttered. "Look, after we eat, and they would be offended if we didn't stay, we really need to be going. I'd really rather Grandfather not send in reinforcements."

"I'd really rather find my grandmother," I replied archly. "So, food first, then continue to run like the dickens?"

"No, I asked, there's a field about a mile west of here where the hunters keep their horses. We can easily steal a few and make better time."

I cleared my voice pointedly.

"What?"

"Yes, I've taken lessons a few times, but what about the others."

Ivan held up his hands. "I've ridden on the carousal."

"Crap," said Cameron. "We can strap you on if it comes to that, but they're our best bet, and with you and me, Cuz, we won't be stopped if we have them. Every world creates a void for us to fill. No one will ask questions. Gah, you don't ride," he muttered, stalking away. Jackie was busy talking to locals, but her eyes followed him all the same. I leaned into Ivan and nodded my head towards the two of them.

"He doesn't realize he's making it harder on himself. If he were an easy target, she'd dump him."'

"Like Mark and Stephen?"

"Oh, did she date them here too?"

"There? Yes, she did."

"Specificity."

"It's your world, I'm just along for the ride."

"Thank you," I whispered softly. He turned to watch me, his brows knit in confusion.

"For what?"

"For being you."

"In the last week you've called me an ass and an idiot. Now you're thanking me for that."

I rolled my eyes and sighed. "You know what I mean."

"Maybe, maybe not. After all, are you thanking me for being the me of my world, or for being the me of your world, or for both?"

"Okay, forget it," I said getting up, "I changed my mind, you're an ass."

He caught hold of my hand and pulled me back down. "I'm sorry, Princess."

I sighed and relaxed onto the wooden seat. "No you're not. You're just upset you got me riled up enough to leave. If I stay, you're just going to try again."

He chuckled and reached over to push a strand of hair behind my ear. "Ah, but it's so much fun."

"For you, yes."

"I won't deny that."

He gently cupped my cheek, and my breath stopped. I had never been kissed, had no idea what to expect, and was terrified but at the same time excited that Ivan of all people was going to educate me.

"Food time," said Cam, banging a bowl down in front of both of us. I jumped and with the exception of my father, I had never wanted to swear at someone more. "Here, Cuz, Ivan, you can get your own."

Ivan dropped his hand with a sigh and a wry twist of his lips before going off to do just that.

"You have funny taste in friends," said Cameron as he spooned the stew. "Both of those two are Seers. They can pick us out of a crowd with a dozen look-a-likes and you attract them like a bee to honey."

"What is so wrong with that?" I asked, blowing on mine to cool it.

"In other worlds, they don't like us much," he replied. "In fact, if we run into any here, we're probably in for a rough go of it. We used to be burned as witches. In some worlds, we still are, and it was the Seers who showed them where to light the match."

"Well, Mr. Optimism, I trust Ivan with my life. I wouldn't worry about him."

"What about the other one?"

"I don't know, but she's here, so we might as well accept our fate and look at the bigger picture."

"You mean like the fact that your Seer doesn't ride?"

"Hey, I barely ride. My father was too busy to take me anywhere, and my mother was terrified of horses. Does Jackie ride?"

"As a matter of fact she does, so we'll have to keep track of the two of you."

Jackie joined us next, taking the seat across from Cameron. "They're really friendly here," she said as she took a bite. "Bread?"

Apparently Jackie had made more friends than Cameron. I happily took a chunk. A few locals filled in around us, but most of them were children, far too occupied with their own doings to care what we were up to. Ivan was the last to join us, rolling his eyes at his placement next to Jackie, but she barely acknowledged him. In fact the only indication she gave of him being next to her was to lift her nose ever so slightly.

"So, do we know what direction we should be going?" she asked. "North, South, East, West?"

"West," I said without thinking. They all looked to me and I shrugged. "Annie, the lady that showed us in, she said the nearest site of industry is ten miles west. That was what I saw in the mirror, so it's as good a place to start as any."

"We should have had weeks, not hours," muttered Cameron. "We'll never make this."

"Then we keep going and they try and follow," I replied sharply. "You can go back if you want."

"You'll be missed," he snapped. "You all will be missed, and then what? There will be a man hunt and how do we explain that?"

"I won't be missed," I said. "I left a note this morning, and even if either Celeste or my father notices I'm gone for more than a day, which isn't likely, they are even less likely to come after me."

"But your father is a Walker."

"Yeah, that means nothing."

He sighed and looked to the other two. Ivan shrugged. "I told my mom I might be gone for a few days. She asked a lot of questions, but she was pretty good about not expecting answers."

We all looked at Jackie.

"Well, obviously I'll be missed. I didn't think I'd be here this morning, though it'll probably take my parents a day or two to miss me and even that will probably be more from a call from the school than any concern."

Cameron looked between the two of us. "You two have some dysfunctional families."

"Your point?" I asked.

"He doesn't have one," replied Jackie with an equal edge. "People who grow up in a nice family just don't get why some are so screwed up." She blushed faintly and glanced to Ivan. "Sorry for yours."

Even Cameron knew to keep his mouth shut as Ivan was forced to acknowledge her. Slowly, he set his spoon down and met her tentative gaze. "As I've been reminded lately, it's not your fault. You said it yourself, your father's a bastard."

"I did," she said with an eager nod of her head. "Does this mean you'll actually acknowledge me now?"

"Why would you want to be acknowledged by me? You're the popular one."

"Besides the fact that it would upset my dad royally? You seem like a nice guy. And I happen to like people in general."

I had to hide my smile. Ivan was too flummoxed to manage anything but a nod. With a sigh of relief, Jackie went back to eating and so did the rest of us.

THIRTEEN

One of the children was designated to be our guide. Among other things, it seemed these villagers didn't much care for the hunters and were only too happy to help us again. The girl led us to an outcropping where we could see the horses tied in long lines strung across what had once been streets. The lines were secured in the remnants of windows. I couldn't help the shiver of apprehension.

As Cameron knew the most of what he was doing, he went down, pulling Ivan along with him. I figured he thought someone from the Village could help him sneak past the guards. Our guide left when I wasn't looking, and I was left alone with Jackie. She shivered and hugged herself.

"Do this often?" she asked.

"Hardly. You ride?"

"Yeah, it was a valuable life lesson my parents thought was necessary. My sister is the really big horse person, but I can get around one. You?"

"A few lessons over the years, but not really."

"Ivan?"

"Not at all."

She nodded. "Well, this should be fun. I swear, it feels like I'm either stuck in a really weird dream or a video game. Who comes up with this stuff?"

"Beats me," I replied, repressing a shiver from the cold. We sat in silence for several moments. She crawled closer to me, and we huddled together for warmth. Finally, we heard the soft sound of hooves on turf.

"Nora, come on!" Cameron called out in a carrying whisper. I pulled Jackie up and we headed towards the horses. Cameron made quick work of getting the both of us mounted. Jackie adjusted her stirrups and sat back with a natural seat to watch the rest of us. Ivan was still uneasy, and it took the offer of Cameron's assistance to get up for him to break down and climb up on his horse under his own power. "That's the smoothest one we have," said Cameron quietly. "Hold onto the horn, I'll take her reins. Try not to fall off, I don't think if we're spotted we'll be able to come back for you."

"Comforting," muttered Ivan, doing as he was told. Cameron rode up on his gelding and took the split reins from Ivan's horse. Cameron looked back at Jackie and me.

"I guess Jackie gets to look after you, Nora."

I nodded, starting to feel a little queasy. It had been close to two years since I was on a horse. I patted my gelding and prayed for patience from him.

"Ready?" asked Jackie, bringing her mare beside mine.

"As I'll ever be." She looked over at Cameron. "It'll be easier to go straight to a canter," she said.

"Save the trot for later when we have time for lessons."

Cameron gave a curt nod, dragging Ivan's mare up one side of the hill. We walked the horses through the ruin of the town, careful to keep far from the encampment. I wanted to ask how they had managed to steal four horses with no one the wiser, but I was too afraid to speak.

Finally, when we had cleared the last of the outlying buildings, Cameron turned in the saddle and gave a nod to Jackie. She angled her mare directly beside Ivan's and when Cameron set his horse to a canter, she pressured Ivan's mare into doing the same. I was left in their dust, but my gelding didn't want to be left behind, and in seconds I was reduced to holding on for dear life. After half a mile or so, I managed to remember vital pointers, and slowly I got my seat back under me. It was rough, I had certainly not been given the smoothest horse, but he sure was quick. We had caught the others, and even while I struggled not to look like a ridiculous green horn, he started to lead the charge. I hurt just about everywhere when Cameron pushed his horse in front of mine and signaled for us to stop. Another thing my gelding did really well was stop. If not for the horn, I would have been on the cold ground and hoping the grass had broken my fall. Ivan looked ready to be sick, but Jackie and Cameron were glowing.

"We should give them a break, and we're not that far from the outlying buildings." He pointed through a gap in the trees. I squinted, surprised to realize some of the dense objects clouding my view were more abandoned buildings.

"What's the plan when we get there?" I asked, wincing as I shifted in my saddle.

"There should be a local pub or something similar open. We need to start asking if anyone has seen Alanna. Like I said, our horses won't be questioned. Even if the hunters follow us, they won't realize these are theirs. The world has adjusted for us to have them."

I nodded. Just like my trellis and my locker. Jackie just shook her head, muttering something about it not making much sense to her. As we walked on, Cameron had to give Ivan back his reins so that he could steer himself into town on his own. There were guards on duty, and they blocked our path as we approached.

"What business do you have here?"

Cameron sighed heavily and frowned at the both of them. "I don't have to explain myself to you."

"New laws around here, Captain, we have the right to defend our land, even from you hunters."

"We're not hunters," Cameron replied with an aristocratic air. Honestly, he should seriously consider working on the stage. "But that is no business of yours. We are here on family matters. Now let us pass."

The second guard pulled the combative one aside. "Let 'em pass. It's obvious they're not hunters. That one can barely sit a horse."

Ivan glared at the guard, but it didn't do him any good. I seriously doubt it even made him feel better. He muttered something in one of his many languages that had the friendly guard laughing.

"Alright, if you're looking for someone, you should try the Santa Ana." He chuckled softly before finishing. "They also have really good fajitas."

"Thank you," said Cameron before pushing on. The guards watched us, and I could hear them chatting long after we had left. We pulled up outside of the place in question. Cars were abandoned on the streets, and hitching posts had been roughly put in place of parking meters. Everyone who passed watched us with suspicion, and I began to doubt Cameron's assertions that we would be fine. At the doorway, he stopped us all and handed out a few coins.

"We'll probably stand a better chance individually. Be on your guard, and try not to say anything too stupid," he saved this comment for Jackie, but she was ignoring him.

"W-what do we d-do if we get in trouble?" I asked, pushing each syllable out forcefully. I hurt, terror was creeping in on me, and I was exhausted. There were simply muscles I never knew I had screaming at me.

"Run," replied Cameron. "Or you could try the high handed method. Chances are if you make up a story about yourself, they'll believe you."

"That's c-comforting," I replied uneasily. He just nodded and let himself in. Jackie followed on his heels. Ivan took a step but waited for me.

"Do you want me to stay with you?" he asked softly. "Would it help?"

"With my s-stutter?" I asked, still shaking. "Maybe. You seem to help me."

"Then let's go." He took my hand and led me inside. It was seat yourself, and Ivan took a booth at the back. Not much had happened in here since the forties, and it showed. The plastic covered seats were patched with something like duct tape, and the lights had reverted back to candles, but the atmosphere was still something similar to an ice cream parlor. A waitress finally came out to serve us, after studiously ignoring Cameron at the bar.

"What can I get you?" she asked.

Ivan pretended to study the menu. "We're new around here, what would you suggest?"

"Well, its Monday, and usually that means meatloaf, but you're running a little late from the crowd, so we're out. Might try the stew."

"What about the fajitas?" he asked.

She visibly brightened. "Ah, so Scotty sent you. Yeah, I can see about that." She looked over at me. I was trying to literally pry my tongue loose, it wasn't working. "And for your girlfriend?"

"The same. Do you have any iced tea?"

"Fresh, every day." She winked at Ivan and I had to fight the urge to laugh at how universal his appeal was.

"That would be great."

"Sure thing. I'll be right back."

He watched me with a trace of smugness as I finally unhinged my jaw.

"You have a way about you," I said caustically.

"It's a gift."

"So it is. Thanks."

"No problem."

"Good thing you can't ride after all," I said.

He laughed and winced. "I don't think any part of my body will be agreeing with you in the morning."

"But we made it in here because of it."

"No offense, Princess, but they laughed at your expense too."

"Oh, what language was that?"

"It was an odd mix of Spanish and something else I couldn't place, but it sounded close to Mandarin. I think those two have some free time on their hands or these people have invented their own language."

"My own little translator," I said with a grin. "What would I do without you?"

"Now that would be a fascinating theory, maybe you would have to create a forty third world: the one without me."

I laughed. "No thanks. I never knew any of that stuff before today," I continued pensively. "Grandmère only told me the basics, sort of the meat and potatoes. She never explained about making more realms or how it was done. She never even told me what my blood does to one. That was an accident. I cut myself on my broken Portal and it fixed itself, but when it was fixed, it only came to your world."

"I think that should be a sign," he said with a playful grin, but he was hiding something behind his eyes.

"Maybe. Probably."

"Would you go back, if you could?"

The seriousness of his tone brought me up short from my first answer. "I would want to know you were okay there. The other you, so, yes, I would want to go back and check. But I'm not sure I can. Jackie's dad is still there."

"He's still in my world as well."

"Not the same, thing. In your world, he hates you. In my world, he hates my father."

I was surprised when the waitress slid two plates on the table between us. "There you are, the house specialty for the lost. If you need it, we have some extra rooms too. They're at the top, and they rely on fires, but the beds are comfortable."

"We'll have to think about that," said Ivan with a small smile. He raised an eyebrow at me, waiting patiently.

"We have a few qu-questions," I said with a frown towards him. The waitress turned to me with a patient smile.

"If I can help," she said, but her words held an edge towards me.

"Have you had any other vis-visitors in t-the last week?'

She narrowed her eyes ever so slightly and took a half step back. "Maybe, who's asking?"

"I'm lo-looking for my grandmother."

She leaned across the table and propped my chin up to catch the light. "You have her eyes.. Yeah, she was in about a week ago. She was looking for one of the monks."

"Monks?" asked Ivan.

"They live up on the hill. It would be the best land for a fortress, and it might give the hunters an advantage, but the monks took it over just after the fall out. They've been there ever since. If you're sick, that's where you go."

"How far is it?" he asked.

"You have horses?" When we both nodded, she continued. "On horseback, it's probably two hours if you push the speed a little. If you walk, it's half a day."

I sighed, collapsing back into my seat. If we left then, it'd be midnight before we made it, give or take as I hadn't seen a clock in hours. All I had to go off of was that my internal clock wanted to go to bed. Ivan watched me carefully before turning back to the waitress. "I think we'll take those rooms you offered. Is there a place for our horses?"

"Sure, it's extra, but the building next to ours was hollowed out and works as a stable when needed. The cars in it only work on Sundays."

I wasn't certain if she meant this as a joke, I wasn't about to make any assumptions about this world. "And our friends?" I asked.

She sighed and propped one hand on her hip. "You mean the one at the bar and the flirt by the fire?"

Surprised at her comment without checking, I looked around only to find Cameron and Jackie exactly where she said they were.

"Yeah, them."

"I suppose. We've got two rooms, maybe a third if Kevin managed to sleep off his hangover in time to get home." She motioned for another waitress. "If you show Tiana where your horses are, she'll take care of them. I'll see about those rooms. But eat first," she said when I tried to get up.

"They're just parked out front," said Ivan.

"Parked?" asked Tiana. "You mean tied?"

"That too. There are four of them."

She nodded. "At this time of night, they're likely to be the only ones left. No one can steer when they're three sheets to the wind. Alright, I'll see what I can do." She slipped out through the front door, and I finally took a bite of our dinner.

"Wow, this is really good," I said, suddenly famished. I tried my best to eat with manners, but I was just too hungry. Ivan managed better than me, and I could tell he was still uneasy. He ate with one eye on the crowd. Jackie finally came over and collapsed next to me.

"Ooh, food," she started tucking in with enthusiasm as well. "I don't think I've ever been so hungry."

Our waitress had been watching and brought another plate to us. By then Cameron had finally given up on being productive, and he was fighting with Jackie for the last bites on the plate.

"We have rooms for the night," I said as I watched them bicker.

"Why?" asked Cameron, coming up with a start and losing out.

"It's at least two hours to the monastery where our waitress thinks Grandmère went. No offense, but it's got to be close to midnight. I hurt, I'm cold, and I want to go to sleep."

He sighed and leaned back against the plastic covering. "I wanted this done before anyone showed up to hold my hand."

"Don't be an idiot," said Jackie, and Ivan and I jumped to hear her. "We just rode ten miles, ran for probably close to two more, and we're all miserable. Your ego can handle someone else coming for us. And it isn't as if we're going to wait for them. Maybe we'll have Nora's grandmother and be back here before they arrive."

He petulantly crossed his arms across his chest and glared at her. "Right."

"And the horses?" Jackie asked us.

"They've got a stable. One of the waitresses is putting them up now."

Cameron glared at me. "And you just trusted them? You'd better hope they didn't call the watch or the cavalry or something. You are all hopeless!"

He got to his feet and stomped off towards the entrance.

"Now who's hopeless?" asked Jackie. "He thinks this world is out to get us and he goes off alone." She got up and ran after him, leaving me speechless.

"I think they make a lovely couple," said Ivan with a wry smile.

"I think so too," I replied. "If they don't kill each other first." I paused, turning back to him. "Should we go check on them too?"

He shook his head. "No, they're fine, and I seriously doubt your cousin's paranoia is based in any reality. We were given a free pass by the sentry. I don't get the impression that the locals like those hunters very much. They find out we stole the horses, we'll probably be heroes."

"I hope you're right."

He shrugged and sat back as our waitress put even more food in front of us. "So do I."

"This is on the house," she said with another wink at Ivan. "Made fresh this evening. When you're done, I'll show you to your rooms."

"Thank you, Victoria."

She smiled, "Wow, you can read that. You are full of surprises." She was blushing and it made me want to kick Ivan under the table and maybe hit him in the open. "Where are the others?"

"They're checking on the horses," Ivan said with another smooth smile. He noticed me glaring at him, and his smile just grew wider.

"Oh, well, they're in good hands with Tiana. Let me know if you need anything more."

"Will do."

When she was safely out of ear shot, I gave in

and kicked him. "You are an indiscriminate flirt."

"Hey, it just got us free dessert. I would think you would be happy about that."

"Huh." I took one of the four spoons and took a bite of the chocolaty cake in front of me. Closing my eyes, I couldn't contain the moan of satisfaction. "Okay, you get a pass."

"That good?" he asked. Taking a bite, he mimicked me unintentionally. "Yeah, it's that good. Maybe I should flirt more often." He laughed at my sour expression and offered his spoonful. "Come on, this doesn't deserve that sort of face."

"No, but you do."

"Aww, Princess, are you jealous?'

I just snorted and took another bite. "Whatever. It's not like I haven't had to put up with you flirting with people all our lives. I should be used to it by now."

The brat was smiling at me. "So, the other me is a flirt too?"

"He's not indiscriminate, though."

"No, but he does have bad taste." He sighed and took another bite. "If they don't hurry, we won't be saving any. If it bothers you that much, I'll try to stop."

"Don't do anything on my account," I replied haughtily. He watched me for a full five seconds before laughing again.

"You're adorable when you're jealous. Oh, look, they made it back and no one died." He shifted over so that Cameron could join him. I held up spoons for each of them.

"This looks good," said Jackie, taking a bite. "It is."

"So, the horses are all good? No authorities

hiding in the stables?" I asked.

"Don't joke about it," replied Cameron sulkily. "Anything can happen in these worlds, you should know that."

"Yes, I suppose so, but still, the answer to the question is?"

"They're fine. And we got a lot out of the girl that was putting them up. Seems the hunters have aligned themselves with the two strongholds that control this area. Anyone who leaves is being hunted now, not just those who ran from the city. The cities are growing, and the countryside is fighting the losing battle by trying to keep everyone in check."

"Sounds pretty bad," I said softly.

"It is, so the sooner we get done here, the sooner we can go back to normalcy."

"That world is not normal to me," I replied gently.

"Then we send you back to yours. You saw the Portals. Pick yours, and I'll push you through it. Are the rooms ready yet?"

He got up to go ask, and Ivan let out a low whistle. "Someone is in fine mood."

Jackie shrugged and finished the cake. "Could be because he's tired, or because he wasn't able to find a conspiracy under a hay bale. He was getting a lot worse when I finally came in."

"He must be lonely," I said almost to myself. "He lives with his grandfather, if that's all he does, he probably doesn't get out much. World Walking can be a release from that, but if he's never traveled with anyone, well…" I trailed off, trying to come up with the words to what I understood better than they did.

"Could explain his want of social skills," agreed Jackie. "Honestly."

"Did you never take anyone with you?" asked Ivan.

"If I had taken anyone, it would have been you," I replied. "But I found comfort in finding friends in the other worlds. I don't mean to sound rude, but it's possible Cameron hasn't made friends on his travels. Maybe Carl's views on our interaction is that Cameron is not to make friends. Grandmère always encouraged me, I think because she knew I was so lonely at home." Ivan and Jackie both took a few minutes to digest this.

"Makes sense," said Jackie at last. "Well, our waitress is coming back and those look like room keys."

Victoria showed us upstairs to the bedrooms that had been remodeled into individual suites. There was a connecting door in the two we had, and she opened it to reveal a muttering Cameron testing the bed springs.

"Sorry, but Kevin is still in the third room. Hopefully these will do."

"They're perfect," Jackie said. "Thank you."

Victoria took one last long look at Ivan before leaving us to our own devices. He nudged me as he went through the connecting door.

"You can't blame me for encouraging her that time."

I just rolled my eyes and contemplated the room I was in. It had antique furniture that had seen better days but had been well kept over the years of service. There was no bathroom. That was apparently at the end of the hall and was for all the rooms, hostel style. The double bed had handmade quilts stacked on it, and was framed by an old carved bedstead. Jackie was busy spreading out the quilts and inspecting the pillows.

"Which side do you want?" I asked her, coming to take her cast off pillows.

"Either, I'm not picky, but I do tend to toss. So I apologize in advance."

"No worries, I snore."

She smiled wryly and came over. "Can you help? That nice lady helped me put this thing on, but I don't get how it works."

"Yeah, I think Cameron will be forced to dress us all tomorrow. Let me see what I can do." We were both down to our tunics and in bed in less than five minutes. Jackie yawned as she snuggled into the thick cotton sheets.

"I should have brought contact cleaner. Who would have thought I'd be sleeping in them? Nora?"

"Yeah?"

"I think I'm okay if I wake up and this isn't a dream, but if I start screaming tomorrow morning, I apologize in advance."

"No problem. I'll keep that in mind."

"Good, night."

"Good night, Jackie."

I was amazed by how quickly she dozed off. I noticed that the lights were still on in the other room, and I cautiously got out of bed to check on the boys. Cameron, likewise, had quickly fallen asleep. Ivan was still busy trying to get the vest off.

"Need help?" I asked softly.

"That would be nice."

"Hold still." I had finally figured the secret to this things when taking Jackie's off. There was a double knot at the top to keep the sides evened, and as long as that was loosened first, it was easy after that. "There you go."

"Thanks, Nora." He dropped it on the ground, glaring at it. "I still don't understand what was so wrong with cargo pants."

"At least they still have zippers on the pants."

"That really makes no sense when you look at this thing," he kicked it with his foot.

"Have you seen fashion in your world? It doesn't make sense either. I mean, why buy a pair of pants with holes in them?"

He smiled and moved around the offending article. "What, they don't have that in yours?"

"Oh they do, and a few other equally ridiculous things, but I haven't exactly been reading up on your fashion magazines to give any more examples."

"You should work on that." He frowned at Cameron as he blew out the extra candles until both rooms were down to one a piece. "Your cousin is a bed hog."

"So's Jackie."

"Next time we should make them share."

I giggled, shoving my fist in my mouth to stop. "That's so bad," I whispered as Cameron rolled over. "I think my sensibilities have been offended."

"Really? Then I shouldn't point out that would leave us to share a bed."

I blushed, and even in the meager light, I knew he could tell. "Stop it."

"Alright, but just so you know, I hurt too bad to even roll over. I think it's going to take more than one person to get me out of bed tomorrow. And all of you to convince me to get back on that horse."

"I'm not sure I'll be any better," I replied. "But hey, what's another two hours?"

"Four, Princess. Two up, two back, and then no doubt we'll be forced to ride back towards the Portal. When we get back to our world, I think I'll never walk again."

"Hmm, we'll have to find a wheel chair for you then."

"Smart ass."

"I learned from the best."

He smiled and shook his head at me. Reaching over, he kissed me on the top of my head. "Good night, Nora."

"Good night, Ivan."

I limped back to bed, his mention of sore muscles reminding me of just how bad everything below my waist hurt. The bed was soft enough to fall into, but if it hadn't been for my all out exhaustion, I might have had issues will how little space had been left to me. I barely managed to roll over before finally, blessedly falling asleep.

FOURTEEN

Sunlight was shining brightly thorough the window when I managed to pry my eyelids open the next morning. Sitting up, my body cried foul, and I managed only to prop myself up against the pillows. Jackie stirred beside me, muttering incoherently until opening her eyes.

"Where are we?"

"You're in a dream," I replied, trying to get my brain up to functioning speed. "You'll wake up from it tomorrow."

"Nora?" She pushed herself up and fell back against the bed frame. "That was all real?"

"Depends," I replied. "How do you want me to answer that?"

"Truthfully. Are we really in a world that has no cars, cell phones, or electricity?"

"Yes."

"Ugh." She crawled back down the bed and pulled the covers over her head. "And that means we still need to ride today. Any chance we get home by dinner?"

"I don't know."

"You're not very helpful."

"What do you want?" I asked blearily. "It's too early in the morning to think."

"It's actually pretty late," said my cousin, coming to stand in the doorway. "After nine, in fact. You two are holding us up, so get dressed. Ivan and I will be down getting the horses ready. There's continental style breakfast down stairs. My suggestion is try the biscuits."

"And I thought I hated him last night," muttered Jackie. "He's even worse in the morning."

I grunted in agreement and stumbled out of bed. In the light of day, my brilliant break through was dulled, but after two failed attempts, I managed to pull the vest contraption on. By the time I was done, Jackie was ready for hers. Wearily, we made our way down the stairs. Every step hurt, but the lure of food was too great to hobble me too badly. Jackie and I ate with relish, the food was just as wonderful as the cake. The lady on duty seemed to be the owner, and she treated us with every civility. As we finished up our food, Cameron came back in for us.

"You two are slow," he said darkly. "Come on, we need to be going. As it is, someone in my family is no doubt on their way here."

"Oh, we have more family members?" I asked.

"They're not related to you. My mother is a Walker as well as my father. Seriously, let's go. I already got that city slicker up, now it's down to you."

"That's harsh," I said, limping past him. "What insult do you have directed at me?"

"Not nearly as many as he has for me," replied

Jackie with an arrogant toss of her head. "Don't worry, I'll help you get on."

Muscles I barely even knew I had screamed as I got onboard my horse, and the only reason I knew of their existence was because they hadn't stopped groaning since the day before. I had decided to name my horse Philippe for the big draft in *Beauty and the Beast.* He didn't match the color or conformation, but he did have a blaze like Philippe. I swear he rolled his eyes at me as I gingerly climbed aboard. Cameron was in no better a mood than when we had gone to sleep, and as soon as we were off the streets and headed towards the monastery, he set his and Ivan's horses to a full out gallop. I whimpered and asked Philippe for the same. He didn't need me to ask, he quickly took off to match the others. The ride the day before hadn't tempered his speed. He seemed almost happy to be running so fast. I felt tears welling in my eyes as I held on, staying low and out of the wind. Riding a horse is not quite like riding a bicycle. It might be the same concept, once you've learned you don't really forget, but the muscle memory required to stay seated on a horse was half the battle. I didn't know how Ivan was managing to stay on, and Jackie seemed to have taken our side in this conflict, riding hard alongside Cameron and arguing over the wind. This time, when we came to an abrupt halt, I wasn't so lucky as I had been the night before. Philippe didn't go anywhere, but that didn't really make matters better.

"Nora! Are you okay?"

Three voices were calling out to me, and it hurt to think that far from my body. I had managed to hold onto the saddle and slow my fall, but it had still been an impact with an immovable object. Slowly, I sat up, surprised to find Ivan helping me.

"How are you going to get back on?" I asked him.

"I'll manage. At least you know who we are."

"I don't think my head was the primary point of contact. Ack, I have to get back on now."

"We can stand to wait a few minutes," said Jackie sharply, still glaring at Cameron.

"I hold no responsibility because you two can't ride."

"Shut up, Cameron," I said miserably, letting Ivan help me to my feet. "When someone is in pain is not the time to be so incredibly rude."

He just rolled his eyes and wheeled his horse away, Ivan's still in tow.

"Nora, are you going to be alright to ride?" asked Jackie, corralling my errant mount.

"I think so. My butt will beg for mercy, but most of me already was."

She handed my horse back over. "We should try walking for a little. I ride a couple times a week and I hurt. I imagine Mr. High and Mighty does too, but he won't admit it."

I don't know how Ivan or I did it, but somehow we managed to get back on, and as long as we were walking, I wasn't crying. After too short a break, Cameron gathered Ivan's mare back up to him and we set off at a brisker pace. This time, though, we were allowed to pace ourselves with frequent walk breaks. Just as the sun was reaching its zenith, the monastery came into formidable view.

Sitting on top of a hill, it easily towered over the rest of the area. The trees had been cleared up the road, throwing the stone work into sharp contrast. Whoever had come up with the design had clearly seen those imposing monastery's set in the most improbable areas in Europe and Asia. There was no mountain cliff to cling to, but every angle seemed to grow from the hill itself. It wasn't as though some unimaginative person had plopped a building down in the middle of nowhere. This took planning and a little bit of imagination.

We were not the only people at the base of the hill. Pilgrims were waiting in lines for the carts to take them up. I could count four such carts, and they seemed to act like ski lifts. Cameron ignored the lines and set his gelding up the side of the hill. I felt like I was cutting in line, but my horse didn't give me a chance to feel guilty, plowing after Cameron with purpose. Two monks stopped us at the top, holding out their arms and warding off even the most eager of horses.

"No horses within," said one.

I was afraid to get off, for fear of what would happen. As I struggled to swing my leg over, my other gave out, and I started to crash down. Cameron caught me and set me back on my feet.

"Come on, you and I need to be the ones to do this."

With a glance at the others, I noticed Ivan was still seated. Jackie was holding his horse as well as ours from the ground.

"What is your purpose?" asked the monk who had stopped us.

"We are looking for a family member," replied Cameron.

"You are in the wrong place for that, young master," replied the other. "This is a place for miracles."

"Well, then we need a miracle," I replied. Both monks looked at me, and one leaned in and squinted at me first, and then Cameron.

"She said someone would come for her," he said to the other monk. "Come, child, we will take you to where you need to go." He called out in yet another tongue I didn't understand and two more monks, or whatever a monk in training was called, came bounding forward to take our horses. Ivan was finally forced to get off, needing a minute to steady himself before slowly making his way to us. We were led past the main courtyard where the pilgrims were being treated. Through a set of arches, we came into a magnificent courtyard. Bright tiles lined a shallow pool where fountains sprang. On either side of the pool were orange trees, and at the end of this all was yet another arch way. I walked by in awe, nearly running into an orange tree. Within the next set of doors, we came into a much smaller courtyard, this one a heptagon with roses all around the borders.

"Wow," said Jackie, speaking for all of us. "I've never seen anything like it."

"Thank you," said a woman's voice. We all jumped slightly as a slender matron came down the steps at the end of the courtyard. Her robes were a bright purple, contrasting sharply with the brown of the monks who led us. Her face was pale, framed by black hair and set with brilliant sapphire eyes. She looked like a creature from mythology, sent to tempt men and then kill them. "I have held them as a source of personal pride. When I came here, the architecture was there, but a building is not a home until it can speak for itself." She bowed her head slightly as one of the monks whispered in her ear. Stepping back, her eyes went directly to me. "So, you are Alanna's family? How sweet. I think she anticipated a greater turn out."

I shivered at the scrutiny and her tone. "Is she here?"

"Of course," replied the woman. She flicked her pale hand at the monks, and they went scurrying. "I brought her here. But she failed me."

Ivan reached out and took my hand, squeezing reassuringly. I squeezed back, amazed to find that my tongue had not failed me yet. "How so?"

"She said she could save my son, but she only succeeded in trapping them both. Now I have no one to free my son, and she deserves her fate within those confines."

"What is wrong with your son?"

Her blue eyes sharpened, and she came to stand mere inches from me. "He's like you, I imagine. You have the same aura of difference." Her gaze flicked to Cameron but came back to me. "Yours is nearly as strong as his. Would you like to see Alanna?"

"Of course."

"Then come." She spun, her robes flowing gracefully out and back around her as she led the way deeper still into the monastery's confines. Dozens of men were busy with the gardens. As far as I could see, she was the only woman here. We passed through enclosed rooms, and here the monks were studying. Finally, after forcing aching muscles up two flights of stairs, we came to a halt in a tiny garret. It was completely empty save for one mirror on the far wall. "There she is. I'll give you a few minutes to yourselves."

Without waiting for her to shut us in, I walked over to the mirror. There was no other world shining back at me, just a shimmering reflection, like molten silver. Cameron stopped beside me, and shook his head.

"I've never seen anything like it," he whispered. "That's not another world. It's this world, only in limbo. Literally, it's like the fabric of this world has been caught in this distortion."

I reached out a hand, but he caught it quickly. "No, Nora, if you go through there, you'll be trapped too."

"But how did she get that message to me? Somehow you have to be able to get back out."

"Not necessarily," said Ivan quietly. "She could have sent that note knowing what she was doing. I don't think I was the only one to notice our hostess is not exactly warm and fuzzy."

"She's my aunt," said Jackie.

"What?" All three of us said at the same time.

"I mean, clearly, this is another world, but she is definitely Violet Elliot Biden. My father's sister. Well, one of his sisters. My grandfather got around. Last time I checked, we know of six half siblings." She glanced at me and then back at the mirror. "Violet was the piece of work. She tried blackmailing my dad when I was just a baby. No one really talks much about it, but he got her to join his campaign team instead, and I guess they get along now."

"Does that mean you might be able to get us out of here?" asked Cameron.

Jackie shrugged. "I don't know what you mean by that. I'm surprised she didn't recognize me, but that's fine by me, too. But if you're wondering if her affection for my family might help, that would be a no."

During my crazy ride and my painful fall, the cut on my finger had worked its way open again. While Cameron was busy with Jackie, I reached out with my thumb and laid it on the glass. A loud boom sounded and we all jumped. The door behind us opened, but I couldn't turn away. As I stood there, bleeding into the mirror, I saw it begin to take shape. However, there was no real world flashing before me. It was my own past, literally, flashing before my eyes. Behind the screen, I could see a boy, no older than Ivan's middle brother. He was holding up his hand as if controlling the camera reel. When he could see me, he dropped his hand, and suddenly we could all see him as distinctly as if he were standing on the other side of a glass door. He had his mother's features, from the pale skin to the black hair, but his eyes were suspiciously gray. Glancing nervously at Cameron, I could see his recognition as well. Were gray eyes with a hint of purple that rare? Maybe they were, maybe they weren't, but considering how many of us could World Walk, the probability of very many having our eyes and not being related was astronomical.

Behind him, my grandmother came into view. She placed her hand on the boy's shoulder, and then met our gazes. As she moved, the reflections rippled, like seeing something through ripples. Even through the murky reflection that was imperfectly stable, I could see her tense. Her mouth moved, but I couldn't hear a word she said. Beside me, Cameron had pulled off one of his tools and had pricked his finger. When he put it on the mirror, I caught a few glimpses of his life before the boy within controlled the mirror itself. This time when the image settled, we could see both the boy and Alanna clearly.

"Alinora, whatever you do," said my grandmother, her voice suddenly clear, "do not come through here. It is too unstable."

"What is this world?" asked Cameron.

"It is Andre's world. He is not grounded enough to have created a full world, it is why we're still here. I had wanted your father here, Nora. He knows the most about crossing into such realms." Her hand tightened on the boy's shoulder. "And Nora, dear, I would like you to meet your brother."

I staggered, nearly falling away from the mirror, but Ivan caught me. "What?"

She smiled coldly. "I came here for him, and no doubt your father has a great many questions to answer when I see him again."

Ivan reached around me and snapped my jaw shut.

"Which Ivan is this?" my grandmother asked.

"Sorry? Oh, the Thirteenth Realm."

She nodded. "Good. Now, say hello, Nora, and be polite."

"Hello Andre," I said weakly.

He waved, but any movement by him made the world ripple. "Hello Nora, Grandmère has told me a lot about you."

I smiled weakly, not sure what to say. "So what do we do?" I asked instead.

"I don't know. As you can see, your blood can stabilize, but it takes both of you to make it as open as it is. No one can cross."

"That's not right," argued Cameron. "If one of

us puts our hand through, so long as it's bleeding, it'll keep the Portal open. You should be able to get through."

Grandmère shook her head. "The second Andre moves, what you see will alter. He was too young to make this."

"What about one of us?" asked Ivan, motioning to Jackie. "If the portal's open, we should be able to cross, right?"

She frowned mightily. "If I add my blood, it might be enough. But if it doesn't work, you'll be trapped here as well."

"I'm willing to try," said Jackie. She glanced at me with a small smile. "He's my cousin, after all."

"Can you get me a sharp object?" asked my grandmother. "I have nothing to open a wound with."

Ivan pulled out his tool of all trades and handed it across the Portal. He jumped as his hand touched the other realm, and when he pulled back, his arm was still covered in a shiny layer.

Grandmère was shaking her head. "It isn't stable enough," she said sadly. "This won't-"

I cut her off by pulling my hand back. Taking my own tool, and before I could think better of it, I cut straight across my palm. Crying out, I thrust my bleeding palm back through, and the realm cleared instantly. Grandmère's eyes widened in shock. "Nora, that was very foolish, my dear. The mirror will drain you."

"Then we should be quick about this," replied Jackie briskly. Before anyone could say anything more, she walked across the threshold. I began to feel what my grandmother had been talking about. I was weak from the draining. Ivan wrapped his arm around my waist and held me up. Behind us, people were gathering, but I could scarcely focus. I was just beginning to think that passing out might not be such a bad idea when Jackie came back through with my brother in hand. My grandmother slipped through, and she wrenched my bleeding hand from the mirror just in time. As I pulled back, it shattered into so many pieces, no amount of blood would repair it. Surprised, but woozy, I collapsed to the ground, helped by Ivan, as the people outside came rushing in. I was too light headed to notice what was going on, all I could make out were squeals of happiness, and they weren't all from Violet. I was helped down the stairs and laid out on a bed. Slowly, I dozed off.

When I came to, I was alone. Sitting up, I found that I still hurt and it had only gotten worse with rest. Looking at my hand, I was impressed by the professionalism of the wrap. Swinging my feet over the side of the divan, I tried to get to my feet, but my head swam too much, and I sat back down with a small cry. The door opened slightly, and Jackie looked in.

"Oh, good, you're awake." She slipped in and hurried over to me. "You'll never believe what is going on out there."

"No," I said, rubbing my head. Now that part of me hurt.

"It's like a family reunion for me out there. All four of my father's half sisters are here. Turns out the leader of one of the clans is my grandfather. Get this, the leader of the other is my father. All my aunts and uncles came here twenty years ago and took over the monastery as a safe haven for the sick, sort of like a red cross station for the innocent casualties."'

"Does that mean you exist here?" I asked wearily, still struggling to think clearly.

"No. Only my sister. My mother died here giving birth to her. He remarried, of course, and has four more kids, but I don't exist."

"Wow, that's kind of crazy."

"I know, right? Anyway, Violet has decided we are to stay here as her honored guests until you recover. She is ready to adopt you for saving her son. When Alanna told her who you are, that just made Violet want to keep you more. Apparently, well, I don't think I should tell you that."

"What, how my father cheated on my mom? Mathematically speaking, that's what had to have happened. I'm struggling with a good character trait of his right now."

"Oh, no, Violet seduced your dad. Apparently he used to come here with your mother for the medicinal purposes."

"My mom World Walked? Wow, things you would think your parents would share."

Jackie shrugged. "I have no expectations when it comes to parental responsibility. Anyway, Violet fell hard for your dad, so when he came here alone, she seduced him after possibly drugging him. Nine months later, welcome Andre. He never came back afterwards, but she still thinks kindly of him."

"Amazing, isn't it?" I asked bitterly. "How does someone like my father even deserve to have two people pine over him?"

She patted my arm consolingly. "Really, when we get back, you need to meet my family."

"Or not."

"Or not, but I promise, they're just as messed

up as yours."

The door opened again, and this time it was Ivan who came through. Jackie jumped up and hurried out. "I'll tell your grandma you're up."

Ivan smiled at me and took a seat beside me. "How are you feeling?"

"Like I fell off a horse. Oh wait, I did."

"If you want, they'll give you a nice massage with scented oils. It works wonders."

I sniffed experimentally. "Apparently."

He laughed, picking up my bandaged hand in his. "I wouldn't be surprised if this heals faster than modern medicine, either. Those monks know what they're doing."

"So, how's it going out there?"

"It's an impromptu party, even Cameron is being forced to enjoy himself. After all that fear and apprehension about Violet, she has just become the nicest person. Cameron, though, has to find a negative, and pointed out that if we had failed, she might have killed us."

"Life of the party he is."

"Yeah, anyway, everyone here's been great. They've fed us, taken care of our aches and pains, and they are, as we speak, arranging to take us back to the Portal we came through. Violet assures us that with an escort of monks, no one will stop us."

"Wow, I can see where everything working out would really rankle Cameron."

"Yeah, he wants to sneak off into the night after breaking us all out of jail cells. Got to give him credit, though, he has an imagination. I mean, he was positive they would poison us with the drink or the oils, or the medicine on your hand. Definite case of paranoia."

I laughed softly and leaned back. "Never a dull moment."

"With you? You're right. Not a one."

FIFTEEN

Violet was true to her word. We received a full escort back down the hill. Ivan and I were allowed to ride in the cart rather than face another day in the saddle. The hunters in question came out to watch us pass, but, again, Violet had been right, they didn't touch us. Cameron, still paranoid, had the monks drop us off a mile from the Portal, and only Violet and Andre followed us up the hill. Cameron started to get twitchy towards the top, but Grandmère ignored him, helping Andre up the climb. Andre truly loved my grandmother, he talked almost non-stop to her, and I began to feel sorry for the inevitable departure that was coming. The stake Cameron had left was still in place, and we could easily tell the edges of the Portal. One by one we thanked Violet and she thanked us, hugging me to the point I couldn't breathe.

"Thank you, so much for giving my son back to me," she said with tears in her eyes. I nodded mutely, not sure what to say. "If you ever come back here, please come see us." She turned to my grandmother. "I plan to take you up on your offer,

Alanna, when he is a little older."

My grandmother nodded, hugging the other woman. "Usually when they're twelve they can begin to control their gift. He could World Walk now, but he can't be allowed to experiment"

"Then we'll be seeing you soon."

This last comment brought me up short, but Ivan had been watching out for me and pushed me through. It was so foreign to land back in a world more familiar. I looked around, blinking in surprise as the light bounced off of the cartons and lit up the mirrors. Grandmère was the last through, and she frowned mightily at our location.

"You came to Carl to get you through?" she asked me sharply.

"As opposed to what?" I asked in frustration. "Honestly, why is it complete strangers thank me better than my own family? And for that matter, complete strangers remember my birthday better than my family."

She pointed her finger at me. "Alinora, there is no need to get lippy. You knew from my letter I wouldn't be here on time. If you had just asked your father, I might have made it in time."

"Ha! My dad's too busy with my mom, version 2.0. And in my world he's got her dad after us," I said, gesturing to Jackie.

Grandmère's face froze, and she looked back at me carefully. "What do you mean by that?"

"Which part?"

"Alanna? Is that you?" Carl came limping around the corner. "I thought I heard your dulcet tones. Oh, good, you're all back." He came up to his grandson and hugged him. "I was expecting you yesterday."

"I know," Cameron said in a near whine, "I did the best I could."

"I know that, boy, why do you think I didn't send anyone in after you?"

"You see?" I cried to no one in particular. "Why can't I be greeted like that?"

Ivan came and took hold of me. "Easy Princess, come on, we should really be getting back to the mainland. If we hurry, we can make the evening ferry. I'm sure half the Village will be waiting for us dock side."

"Oh, no!" exclaimed Jackie. "What if my family is there?"

"Jackie," said Ivan, and his direct address was so new as to be startling. "Do you honestly think anyone would look for you on Finch Island?"

"No, good point. I like your plan, Ivan," she said with a tentative smile. He smiled back and I do believe it was the first time they had ever shared a kind word for each other.

"Thanks. Hey, Cameron! Do you have anything for Jackie to wear back to the main land?"

Cameron sized up Jackie and nodded. "Yeah, I'm sure we do." He clasped her upper arm and drug her behind a row of crates. Ivan grinned from ear to ear.

"Perfect couple."

I just shook my head at him. It took a little wandering before I finally found my clothes. I desperately needed some clean clothes and a shower, but it was so wonderful to be free of that vest contraption forever. Cameron came with Jackie to take us to the ferry, but my grandmother wasn't done with me.

"Alinora, we still need to discuss matters."

"Grandmère, the only boat off this island leaves in, what twenty minutes?"

Cameron checked his watch. "Eighteen."

"Eighteen minutes, so, if you don't mind, I'd really rather get home and discuss this later. Besides, I really think you should talk to my father first. And I would pay to be there."

She frowned at me. "Don't take that tone of voice with me."

I just shrugged. "I'm sure your brother, who you never told me about, would be happy to find you a room here for the night."

She snorted angrily and stalked after us. "When I'm finished with your father, I will be speaking to you."

"I know."

She narrowed her eyes at me, but didn't say another word all the way down to the docks. Ivan was the one to get us all onboard in time for departure. The trip was quiet, but at least this time we didn't have to hide in the hold. We were given more than one sideways glance, but Grandmère had a certain air about her, and no one wanted to bother her, especially as she looked ready to lay into someone. I just hoped most of the anger got to be directed at my father and that I would come out on the lesser end of the hurricane.

Jimmy was on the pier when we disembarked. He didn't seem to care if anyone was watching, picking me and Ivan up in a bear hug.

"Thank God, I didn't aid in your deaths! Oh, I can go home now."

I laughed as he finally put us down. "You're a lunatic, Jimmy, we said we'd be alright."

"That was before you were gone for two days.

Where were you?"

"Long story," interjected Ivan smoothly, he guided Jimmy away from the dock with questions about his mother.

"Well," said Grandmère in clipped tones, "it's nice to see you making friends, Nora."

"Thanks." I turned back to Cameron. "Are you coming with us?"

"What? No, I need to get back, Grandfather will be waiting for me."

"You're welcome to come visit."

"I will, but you know where I live, and I don't know how to get anywhere out here. I've been on that island for this realm for the last four years."

"Well then I'll come get you."

"Sounds good, Cuz." He gave me a quick hug. "See you around, Jackie." He nodded politely to her before boarding the ferry again.

She sighed. "He's warming to me," she said. "Can you and Ivan get me back to the buses? I doubt I'd be able to get back on my own."

"Of course. Ivan's got to do this all anyway, I don't know where I'm going."

"Buses?" asked Grandmère. "Don't you have your own vehicle?"

"Not in this world."

She clamped her mouth shut on her immediate answer. "We'll have to see about that." She set off regally, but I was pretty sure she didn't have a clue where she was going. Luckily, Ivan intervened before Jackie or I could catch up. Along with Jimmy, the five of us made our way back to town. We saw Jackie off on the bus that would take her closest to her home. I felt sorry for her and the reaction that was bound to be waiting, but she assured me she'd be alright. That just left the four of us. Jimmy was too intimidated by Grandmère to say a word, and Ivan and I just kept mum to stave off the outburst she had promised. When we got off two blocks from where I now lived, Jimmy stayed on the bus with a look of terror, taking the bus back in the hopes of grabbing another rather than spend another minute in my grandmother's company. Ivan, though, offered her his arm, which she pointedly refused, and stayed with us right up to the front steps.

"Thank you, Ivan," she said coldly, "but I think you had best not come in with us."

He looked to me, and I just shrugged, jerking my head in the direction of the back. He nodded in understanding and made his departure. I made to open the door, but Grandmère pushed me aside. "No, Nora, I want to face this head on, not by sneaking in." Whereupon she rang the door bell.

It was Celeste who opened the door, and it took my grandmother half a second to take her in. "What has my idiot son been up to?" she asked in barely contained fury. "Step aside, Celeste, I need to speak with him."

Her eyes round in fear, she did just that, turning to me in question as I followed Grandmère in.

"Where have you been, Nora?"

"It's a long story," I said guiltily. "You might want to go for cover now."

"Peter!" Grandmère's voice rang across the house, and upstairs, I could hear a definite jump and then a bang. If there had been a Portal anywhere in that house, I was pretty sure my dad would have been using it. Instead, a door opened softly upstairs.

"Mother?"

"No, the Tooth Fairy, of course it's your mother! Get down here this instant and come explain a few things to me."

He slunk down the hall, forty one years old but suddenly reduced to being a naughty toddler. Celeste continued to look between all of us. When Grandmère didn't immediately demand my attendance, I took Celeste by the hand and led her to the furthest corner of the house. We didn't say a word for the next thirty minutes. We would have had to shout to be heard over my grandmother. I felt a tiny pang of sympathy for my father when the storm finally eased. Celeste was looking sick, and holding her belly as though suddenly realizing just what it held.

"Nora!" I jumped, but hurried to heed the demanding call.

"Yes Grandmère?"

"Sit."

I promptly sat.

"Now, your father has attempted to evade a direct answer about coming for me, but I think we have come to an understanding. In case I did not say it sooner, thank you for coming to my rescue. It was foolish, impetuous, but well intentioned and, above all odds, successful." She paused and I knew she was waiting.

"You're welcome, of course."

She nodded, pleased. "I am sorry I did not take a stronger hand in your education sooner. You have a true talent, greater than mine, and certainly greater than your father's. I think you should start to work with Cameron and Carl."

"Oh, okay."

"But before all of that, I have a question for you, something your father never bothered to ask you. Do you wish to go back?"

"To the Twelfth Realm?'

"Yes. We could either go back to Carl's or I could track down where my Portal is in this realm."

"I would like to," I said slowly. "I need to know he's okay."

She raised her white eyebrows. "You mean Ivan?"

"Yes. The other Ivan."

She narrowed her identical eyes at me. "Which do you care for more?"

"Why?"

"I need to know you won't do something stupid like your father if you lose one. You need to stay in the world where your heart is."

I opened my mouth, but I had no answer. "I'd prefer to stay here," I finally said. "There's more here for me than there ever was there."

She nodded, satisfied. "Very well. I do not begin to comprehend the public transportation around here, but I did manage to extract from your cousin that the next ferry is in the morning. Will you be ready?"

"Sure, but what about school?"

"You have already missed two days, another will not hurt anything. But after you shower, I would suggest you let me look at your hand."

"Of course."

"Well, go on my dear. No time like the present."

I was hardly surprised to find Ivan sitting on my bed. He was watching me with shuttered eyes.

"Quite the set of lungs your grandmother has."

"I know, right?" I dug around in the dresser for a clean pair of clothes.

"So, you're leaving tomorrow?"

"Yeah, tomorrow morning."

He got up, not quite meeting my eyes. "Well, since you're home safe, I'll go reassure my mother about my own safety. See you around, Princess."

I reached out to stop him, but he was too quick for me. I had no idea what any of that had been about, and short of following him home, I had no way of finding out today. Instead, I decided to fix what I could, which was mainly just my level of cleanliness.

Grandmère had either borrowed or browbeaten Celeste into the use of her car. Either way, the next morning she and I drove to the docks. She complained bitterly about publicly parking such a nice car, but we didn't have too much time to dawdle. Finding our way back in the daylight was a piece of cake in comparison to my first trip out. Carl and Cameron were even waiting for us at the back entrance. I was bustled into the building, where daylight lit up the far corners better than moonlight ever could. Three people were talking at once, but I was not one of them. Grandmère was very firmly guiding me on, pushing me towards a rippling Portal. Before I could rethink my decision, I was back in the Twelfth Realm.

SIXTEEN

It took me several seconds to blink my eyes in adjustment to the muted colors. I tried shaking my head, but that didn't help. Looking around, I was surprised to find myself two blocks from my school. As it was early morning, I thought the best option to find Ivan would be to make the trek back to school. However, after going to two classes and not seeing him, I finally broke down and stopped this world's Jackie in the hall. She seemed to need a moment to recognize me.

"Nora? What are you doing here?"

"This is a school isn't it?" I asked. "Have you seen Ivan?"

She jerked as if I had slapped her, and I realized I had probably never shown so much backbone in all of our years of acquaintance. "Yes, but you left. So did Ivan. On Monday. His dad got a new job, surely you knew that."

"Of course. Thanks."

This was not what I had expected. Now I had to figure out how to get to the southern half of the state. If I managed to avoid traffic, it was at least a three hour drive. To top off my transportation challenged day, I had to figure out the bus system to get back to my house. Even though the front door was locked, I found the spare and let myself in. Not a lot had changed in the week I had been gone. Whoever else besides Mr. Elliot had come into my house, they had had a fine time trashing it. It made me wonder why the front door had been shut at all. I got my car keys and went back out, feeling like I was trespassing in another world. Amazingly, no one had stolen my car. Folded under the windshield wiper was a piece of paper. I unfolded it and felt my tears well up in gratitude. Not only had this Ivan told me where he moved to, he gave a print out of directions. I had to chuckle, wondering if my other Ivan would have been quite so thorough. Thinking it over on the drive, I had to seriously doubt it.

It hurt to see the grandiose house at the end of my directions. To think that if things had been different, my other Ivan could have been living this life. I double checked the address, and with a sigh, got out of the car.

"Nora!" turning, I was nearly bowled over by Ivan.

"Hey," I returned his hug. "How are you?"

"The more important question is how are you?" he asked, taking a step back to appraise me. "You look good."

"I am." My fingers reached up to touch a yellowing bruise around his left eyebrow. "I'd love to say the same about you."

He winced slightly and I pulled my hand away. "Yeah, even after my parents arrived, Mr. Elliot was still beating in the door. I didn't get out of the way in time, there might have been some flying shrapnel when he finally broke through."

"But that's all?"

"That's it." He held up his right hand that was bandaged. "I had a splinter the size of a Number 2 pencil in here, but nothing else."

I held up my bandaged hand. "I understand." A tiny trace of disappointment flashed through me as he finally noticed my wound. My secret heart whispered that my other Ivan would have noticed that before I had even noticed his.

"Tell me all about it," he said, pulling me into the house. It intimidated me, but Ivan didn't seem to notice. It had always amazed me that he came from such splendor and remained my friend. He had simply been elevated up another step on that golden ladder.

After we were seated and their maid had been dispatched to get us something to eat, I began to tell him my tale. He took it all in, watching like an eager puppy. I trailed off when the maid returned, but he quickly prodded me into talking again after she had left.

"That's just crazy," he said around a mouthful of sandwich. "So your mother is now your step mother? I don't think I could keep all of that straight. And you say I hate Jackie in that world? Weird."

I sighed, he would pick up on that. "She is a much different person there," I said.

"Well, for me to hate her, she has to be worse."

"No, she's actually better. Much more down to earth, less like a diva."

"Hey, you be nice."

"That was nice. I could try for a few other

adjectives if you'd rather."

"No," he grimaced. "I've heard them all before. So, did you like it there?"

"Of course."

"And is your dad back here yet?"

"Ivan, my dad isn't coming back here."

He stopped mid chew and forced a swallow. "So he's staying with your mother who isn't your mom rather than with you?"

"No, I'm going back."

"What?"

"My family is there, I have a baby brother on the way. The Thirteenth Realm is where my life is now."

"But, I'll never see you again."

"Of course you will. I can still World Walk. Besides, I would hate to miss your eighteenth birthday."

He sighed, collapsing into the sofa and still managing to eat with fervor. "I suppose, but I just thought you'd come back here. You're my best friend, Nora."

"And you're mine," I replied gently. "But you had already moved, we weren't going to be able to go to movies on a school night anymore."

"I thought you might come with me," he said quietly. "It would have been so much better. I wouldn't have to lose you, and you'd finally have the family you deserve."

I smiled, swallowing past the growing lump in my throat. "Thank you, you always were the best friend I could have." I reached over and squeezed his arm. "But I think I might have a chance to have that family on my own. Celeste isn't so bad, and Grandmère will be around making my father behave for awhile."

He sighed again, and reached for another sandwich. "Well, what do we do now, then?"

"I imagine much like we were going to have to do, anyway."

"Is there cross world e-mail?" he asked with sarcastic hope.

"No, but I can cross over at any time and send you letters. Old fashion like. I'll see about getting a P.O. Box in this world. And we can always arrange to do something."

"I guess that will have to work," he replied sullenly. "Is there anything I can do to make you change your mind?"

I shook my head slowly. "No."

"Then I guess I should ask you what you're doing for Christmas."

Laughing, I got to my feet and leaned over to kiss the top of his head. "I'll swing by for Boxing Day."

He watched me with the most pathetic expression I had ever seen. Somewhere between a beat puppy and a begging kitten. "I'll really miss you, Nora."

"I know. And I'll miss you."

He got to his feet and hugged me hard. "Write often."

"I will."

He smiled sadly before showing me to my car. I waved one last time and then drove the three hours back home. I parked my car outside where the Portal was and dashed through. Grandmère and Carl were waiting.

"Twenty minutes to spare," said Carl with a wink. "Go on with you, kid, I'll be seeing you soon."

Slightly confused, I smiled all the same and followed Grandmère back to the ferry. We were the last to board, but we had made it.

"Are you alright?" she asked as we drove back home.

"Yeah. Besides, he had moved anyway, and he was really my only friend there."

"Well, then I guess you made the right decision."

"I guess I did."

She smiled at me a bit whimsically, and we finished the ride in comfortable silence. The sun was threatening to set when we parked outside our home. Before anyone could stop me, I got out and bolted down for the Village. I was getting in shape quickly. This time, the run didn't kill me.

"Hold up, Nora, where's the fire?"

I screeched to a halt and turned to face Jimmy, working outside in the fading light with Luis for company. "Where's Ivan?" I asked, still slightly winded.

Jimmy's eyebrows climbed up, and Luis's fell down in a glower. "What did you do this time?" Luis asked gruffly.

"Nothing, but I wanted to see him."

"Poor boy's been moping around all day. His mom kept him home from school, and does he stay in and rest? No, he's been up and down the streets all day. No reason, just wandering."

"But where is he?" I asked, my heart fluttering in my chest.

"Last time I saw him," said Jimmy, cutting over the top of Luis, "he was headed for the park." I took off with Jimmy still yelling. "You'd better be getting home soon, Nora!"

"Thanks, Jimmy!" I waved over my shoulder and kept up my run. I nearly lost my footing turning into the park, but despite the pain in my side, when I saw Ivan with his back to me on one of the swings, I managed one last push. He looked up in surprise when I nearly collapsed beside him

"Nora, what are you doing here?"

"Looking for you, of course," I wheezed.

"But what are you doing here? In this realm?"

"What, you don't want to share your realm with me? If I had known that, I wouldn't have chosen to give up living in a mansion in L.A."

He helped me into the swing beside him, still perplexed. "What are you talking about?"

I sighed, taking two deep breaths to try and catch up. "I chose to stay here. There's nothing for me to go back to there, and here, I have an attempt of a family, friends, and you."

A tentative smile began to play about his mouth. "Really?"

"Really. And I'll have you know, your other version tried to tempt me with a mansion, so you better be prepared to offer something good."

He watched me intently before leaning back and laughing, let himself swing forward. "I can't offer any mansions, but I can offer my mom's cooking."

"Hmm, that's a tough choice."

"Why, does his mom cook?"

"No, hasn't in years. But they have a cook."

"So now I've got to counter a mansion and a cook."

"Yep." I took to swinging back and forth with him.

"Wednesday pot lucks?"

"Another really good counter," I said with mock seriousness. "All that food does have a certain appeal. Still, I think you need a trump card."

"Such as?" he stopped swinging to watch me.

I stopped as well, pulling even with him. "If I tried to tell you I was leaving, what would you do?"

"I'd try and stop you."

"Why didn't you?"

"It was your world, I thought you'd want to go back."

"And if I said this was my world, would you let me go?"

"Not if I could help it."

I smiled and started swinging again. "Then, Mr. Battuta, I think you have won your case."

He chuckled softly still watching me. "That's it?" He reached out and snagged my swing, forcing me to stop. "All I had to do was tell you not to go?"

"All you had to do was make me feel wanted."

"Didn't he?"

I shrugged. "Wanted, yes, but not needed."

"Well, I did tell you that version of me is an idiot." He smiled in satisfaction and started swinging again.

"You did, on multiple occasions. But I think I've called you an idiot."

"Not the same thing at all," he replied blithely. "I'm an expert on my own behavior, you're just a trained observer."

"Right, whatever," I said laughing.

He jumped from the swing after it hit its max

height and stood waiting for me to do the same. It was nice, really, to have something so consistent and reliable. I gave one last good swing and landed beside him. he reached out and steadied me as I wobbled. Top gymnast I was not. "I really am happy you're staying," he said seriously.

"I am too." We watched each other for several moments, silently communicating more than words ever would. In the distance, several people started calling out to us. I recognized Brad and Maria with a few others. Brad called out to us to join them, and Ivan looked back at me.

"Do you want to go?"

"Where are we going? No, you know what, it doesn't matter. I've never just hung out with friends before."

He was obviously surprised at my statement, but he didn't remark on it. Taking my hand, he led me after them. "Then, Miss Terre, I think it's about time you found out."

And so after seventeen years in the Twelfth Realm, I decided to fully embrace the Thirteenth, my new home.

Sneak peak of:

<u>Through the Rabbit Hole</u>

World Walkers Book II

ONE

There is something to be said about being different, but there is so much more to be said for being normal. When I was younger, I loved being different. One of my favorite pastimes was World Walking between the Forty-Two Realms with my grandmother. We were only a handful of what remained of World Walkers - people who could travel the Realms with the help of specially made Portals. For years, my grandmother would take me through the safe Realms, teaching me the ways of our kind. Then, on one fateful night that just happened to be my twelfth birthday, my mother had died in a terrible car crash, and suddenly I lost sight of what normal truly was.

In addition to World Walkers, there are also Seers - people who look right through a World Walker and know in an instant that we are not in the Realm we belong to. Oddly enough, two of my best friends are both Seers, as much as my grandmother and father might not like it. Take it as my teenage rebellion. While my friends were Seers, my father did not have the same luck - he had been hunted across Realms for months before my seventeenth birthday, and even after I had fallen into the relative safety of the Thirteenth Realm to escape those who hunted him, they were never far behind.

After surviving a painfully steep learning curve to re-learn how to World Walk after years of neglect, life had slowly started to head back to those normal waters I missed so much. Then my grandmother had returned - fully intent on picking up exactly where we had left on in my training. Most students actually get a chance to enjoy their vacations, me, not so much. Grandmère didn't even wait until the end of the first day of my winter break to start. I was barely home from a half day before she arrived at our doorstep, refusing to give an inch when it came to her plans for me. Thinking back on the past few months, I found it remarkable that I ever had fond memories of World Walking with her.

The first nine days of my vacation we bounced in and out of the safe Realms. Even though I had been taught from a young age how to World Walk, after my mother's death, my father had refused to let me venture out from the Twelfth Realm. It seemed pure luck that I had even made it to the Thirteenth Realm at all. However, my grandmother was nothing if not determined, and so like a dog with the bone between her teeth, she drug me through Realm after Realm. We would literally explore far enough for my grandmother to ask me a hundred questions and then we would head back. Unless it was too dark, then we would find a room for the night, my evening peppered with yet more question and answer sessions. It was one endless pop quiz. I was never that great at stressful situations anyway, and I could feel my brain start to frazzle. Then came the tenth day of vacation.

We had spent the night sleeping in the Twenty-Ninth Realm in a small Bed and Breakfast. The Twenty-Ninth Realm had met far more resistance during the Industrial Revolution than most history knew. As a result, they were just now getting land lines, and cell phones looked to be a century in their future. I woke up to the provincial sound of a rooster. Roosters don't have snooze buttons. I was not, by nature, a morning person, but my grandmother had been rather strict about our hours. It was hard to stand up against the force that was my grandmother on a good day, but as our time together stretched on, and on, and on, I struggled to even get a word in edgewise. So, despite my own inclinations, I was miserably up with the sun. I was halfway into the rather elaborate donning of a functional corset and more petticoats than had to be necessary when my bedroom door was abruptly opened.

"Oh, good, you're up." She marched over with all the determination of a drill sergeant. With ruthless efficiency, she had me cinched up in no time. I gasped as the stays tightened, reaching out to the bed in support. "We need to be leaving as soon as you're ready."

I weakly nodded, still wondering if it was normal to see double after such a brutal tightening. With shaking fingers, I donned my blouse and put on the stiff overskirt. The boots were button up and took forever, with all the rest of the outfit, I nearly fell over just trying to get them on. Only when I was dressed did I turn my struggle to my wispy hair - it was long, blond, and had a mind of its own. Putting it up in any sort of intricate pattern was beyond me, and as the people of this realm still didn't have pony tail holders, I was left to struggle with hair pins. I will say, World Walking has a way of creating an abundance of appreciation for how people - especially women - survived with their fashions through the ages.

When I was fit to be seen, I gingerly made my way down the stairs in the ridiculous boots. Electric lights were also something of a new invention to the Twenty-Ninth Realm, still seen only in cities, so instead there were oil lamps at each table. I sat down and accepted the offer of breakfast. With the corset on, my eating was limited, but I was still hungry, and I ate everything they brought, meager though it might be. Grandmère came up to me just as I was finishing.

"Are you ready?" Her tone was brusque, a warm bedside manner was not in her repertoire.

"As I'll ever be." I couldn't help it, I rolled my eyes. It was far too early for the headache of being polite anyway.

"Good, then let's go."

I sighed forlornly, knowing any additional time for more food was out of the question. There would be a long walk ahead, and getting it over with was the best option. While World Walkers could only move between Realms by the use of Portals, which to the untrained eye looks like a really fancy mirror, the positioning of the Portals could be difficult to place. I had learned over my vacation that World Walkers were governed by the Order of World Walkers, who theoretically governed how many Portals could exist in each Realm, but it hadn't taken long to realize that such oversight was sorely missing in real world situations. Instead, we relied on markers that had been placed by other Walkers through the ages.

Within the Thirteenth Realm, on an island off the coast of California, my grandmother's brother had set up an old warehouse where Portals had once been made for profit. My Great-Uncle Carl and my cousin, Cameron, had taken to leaving stakes, painted with glow-in-the-dark paint, within ten feet of the Portals they could track to help us find our way home. The Twenty-Ninth Realm was not the easiest place to find any sort of stake. Just outside of town, the natural forests had taken over the roads. We were forced to beat a way through foliage to find our way back to where we had come from. As the trees all around started to look familiar, I began to look for the painted stake, hoping that somehow I wasn't just traveling in circles. Even after months of World Walking, I'd never go so far as to say I had the best sense of direction.

"Over this way," my grandmother called out.

I struggled up a slippery hill. It was winter, and it was wet. I caught myself from sliding all the way down more than once until we finally reached the slope where the stake was placed. At the last moment, though, I lost track of what I was doing and fell on my back. As I was staring up at the sky, ears still ringing, I noticed that the sky was almost purple, and not from the sunrise. My grandmother was not inclined to help me back to my feet, instead, she stood waiting at the Portal - finger pricked, and ready to open into another Realm.

Another useful fact about World Walking is that the Portals close, and all but a Master Portal can only open with a touch of blood. Some stay open all the time by benefit of high traffic use, but that certainly had not been the case as of late with our travels.

"Why was the sky so close to purple?" I asked as we entered Carl's warehouse.

"Why do you think?"

"Grr," I grumbled. "Why c-can't you j-j-ust answer?"

She stopped her march to who knows where to stare at me. "I thought you were over your stuttering."

"Ob-b obviously not." I replied, crossing my arms across my chest.

"You haven't stuttered since you came here."

Knowing simple speech was fast eluding me, I settled for shrugging.

She frowned darkly at me. "Doesn't this world appear differently to you than the others?"

"Yes."

"Has not every world seemed different?"

"Of course."

"And you never wondered why?"

"I wondered. I j-just n-never asked." The stutter had been with me all my life. I had learned to work through it from a young age, and Grandmother was correct, as soon as I had moved to the Thirteenth Realm permanently, it had nearly evaporated unless I was under a great deal of stress.

She tapped the toe of her now outdated boot. "What have you been learning these last few days? Nothing?"

Her insult stung like salt rubbed in an open wound. Granted, the last few weeks hadn't been a walk in the park, but I hadn't thought I had been a total failure. I took several deep breaths to get my thoughts and tongue in order.

"I thought…I thought this was for my own und-d…my own understanding."

She sighed, having finally realized that she had hurt my feelings. "And so it was, but I had hoped you might pick up on few of the intricacies." Her eyes, nearly purple and so like mine, bore into me. "Tell me you've learned something."

"Of course."

"Then what?"

"I don't know!" I was finally goaded into shouting back.

Grandmère threw up her hands and stalked off a ways before turning back to me. "What is this? You're not the girl I've been working with. You're becoming who you were a year ago."

I smarted as if she had slapped me. "We've b-been at th-this for t-two weeks! I s-start school in a few days…" I took a gulp of air, trying to calm down, "and I haven't had a break."

She frowned, but it was clear from her expression that she hadn't heard what I said. "Perhaps," she said to herself, "Perhaps that might work. Alright, we're going back home. Your father should have been married by now."

"What?!"

"I suggested he actually make it official and that it might be easier without you there."

"What?" I repeated. My father and I had never been the typical father-daughter level of closeness. Ever since my mother's death over five years ago, he'd locked himself into a world I rarely had entry to. It had been beyond brutal to realize that he had moved on, largely without me, when he had found new love in the Thirteenth Realm.

"Honestly, Nora, you're starting to sound like a broken record. Though, I'd rather you were an angry broken record than a mealy worm with no opinion of your own."

"I have my own op-pinions!"

"Yes, but you have a regrettable tendency not to share them. Now, you're right, you've been away from home for far too long. We'll go back, let you see your friends, and then we'll try two more Realms before you start school again. Carl is pushing me to have you start making your own mirrors."

"Really?" All of my earlier anger and indignation vanished for a second as I thought of the rare skill that was casting. My cousin, Cameron, had been itching to do his own Portals ever since I had met him, and I had to admit to some curiosity of my own.

"Really, but I refuse to let you do that until I can be sure you can walk between worlds without bringing about more problems than you might solve. Besides, it is policy that you pass your World Walking credentials before you're ever allowed to fully cast. Practice yes, assist others, yes, but truly cast - not so much."

I ground my teeth. My grandmother was a master of only giving the barest amount of details, even after she knew she had piqued my interest. She hurried us both through a change into more modern clothing, but without any sign of Carl or Cameron, we were forced to leave to catch the last

ferry back to the mainland. Finch Island was a
place of industry and long held grudges. It was not
somewhere either of us wanted to be stuck in for
longer than we absolutely had to be.

Coming November 2021

Born in Germany, and raised in the Pacific Northwest, L.E. Gibler has been writing for as long as she has been riding horses, nearly 30 years for both. Weaving together work in the real world with finishing a college degree in Communications from Washington State University, she is now working towards opportunities in publishing her fourteen (and counting) finished works.

Each venture into the world of written words is a step closer to realizing a long standing dream, and each story shared is a step in the right direction.

www.ingramcontent.com/pod-product-compliance
Lightning Source LLC
Chambersburg PA
CBHW071611030726
47598CB00001B/237